MW00438288

Echevarria

Gretchen Skivington

Basque Originals

Echevarria

Gretchen Skivington

Center for Basque Studies Press
University of Nevada, Reno

This book has been published with the generous financial assistance of the Basque Government

The Center for Basque Studies
University of Nevada, Reno
www.basque.unr.edu
© 2017 Gretchen Skivington

Text and cover design: Daniel Montero

Library of Congress Control Number: 2017964173

For Pat Bieter and Gorka Aulestia

1902

Paradise, Nevada. *Argitzailean* . . . within the vigil of light the ghosts have come for her. All is still—the dead they are listening. Now she is ours they whisper.

Agur Ma ... ri ... a gra ... zias
Hail Mary full of grace

In the house of Echevarria candles ring the lacquered casket wet flickering in light. The wondrously fleshed body of Paz Mendi Elizagoyen lies in state on a banquet table awaiting the long journey home; chestnut hair, once bound, is loosed around her like that of a girl. Her family has purchased the ticket; her bag is packed, farewell and tears on the wharf of Le Havre. This girl of seventeen sent to the New World, Paz Mendi, will never see them again (but this she does not know).

She is bound for America now—to Paradise—her passage indentured making her free.

urrutira   so far far away

Then they gathered round the knife-scored board and ate like princes: white bread, ham of Baiona, a delicious stew pot-au-feu. *Comme dessert du gâteau Basque.* Such tears and singing to say farewell forever. *Sister, sister ... Take me. Take me!*

At four a.m. their voices droning, the dead woman's soul still adrift on the sea. The good food and coffee have worn off home neighbors leaving them out with her land-locked at sea. In the hotel parlor of Echevarria's, liminally lit between midnight and fever, the singers grow weary and

> *shift*
> *shift*   *shift*

> *Bai Indietara   yes to the Indies*
> *to the Americas yes ...*

Her women *auzokoak* keep the night watch. Their voices cingulum ring the costly black box that holds her like a prize. Sisters, sisters sing the mysteries (click clack click clack) heaving grieving breathing sisters beat the bones across the casement of her breast hissing *suscipe* into the womb

Ez det	*I shan't*
Ez det	*I can't*
Ez det	*I won't*
Ikusiko	*Ever see you again*

As sealight luminous rises to day, she clutches the satchel to her chest like a promise embracing her brothers for the last time (but this she does not know). Our mother, still born awaiting safe passage, watches the horizon for the ship which will take her to the New World today. In a room on a table in a hotel in Paradise our lady is waiting, the cold baby pressed close to her breast. Out on the sea the rowers are rowing. Take Paz Mendi to paradise. *Oh sister, sister take me, take me.*

(Hush)
the story now beginning
the tale of them
the tale of me

Ixil ixilik in the stillness gather
she, his Paz
he, her Petro
Ixilik egon
listen to meee. . .

Ator, ator mutil etxera
gaztaiña ximelak jatera
chestnuts are roasting on an open fire

Gather round now
listen to their names chain-linked
in a choir of sizzling
their lives hot hidden
beneath the white coals of a deadened fire

This the sea song
This the singing. . .
I am Ramon Bertsolari

txipli, txapla, plun

The Legend of
Pedro Altube

He had cattle and land beyond all wonder
sheep too many to number
but Pedro Altube had no sons...

1902

The 3:05 pulled into the station: the usual herd of dusty
travelers and sloe-eyed immigrants began to descend
like locusts upon the outpost of a town archly called
Paradise. It was a ragtag and weary bunch.

On this particular day, Pedro de Altube Idígoras
stood watch at the depot—at fifty-five, a six-foot-eight
miracle of a man. He summed up the human cargo,
lit a slim Cuban cigar and squinted lazily into the sun
thinking of his daughters in San Francisco. *Or konpon*,
they'd manage. No matter. Even though the present had turned him up shag lonesome (a man needed
a companion, no matter what), the past was always
over—that much was certain. He'd been ridden hard
and put away wet: completely undone. Pedro Altube

had no sons, but Pedro de Altube knew not what was yet to come.

Paradise was a grueling two-day ride from Tuscarora, and on this dog day the westbound train from Salt Lake was fatefully late. There, at the station, high on the platform Pedro Altube spit out the burning fag of his smoke crushing it expertly beneath the toe of his boot, then comforted himself with thoughts of the fortune forty carloads of prime beef would bring.

Suddenly, there on the platform like a vision stood a trip chivvied girl with a cloth label sewn to her breast: "Paradise Nevada Echevarria" it read: this was some kinda package, the fortune cookie chit of benediction and direction rising then falling with her breath. Altube's eyes had no other place to go but up and down and up again-quite unavoidably-at last they fell naturally upon her face: and what a face. Pedro de Altube thought he was all finished with surprises. Yes, man *baietz*.

She was all of seventeen: just a servant girl indentured by her family to set them free. *Eldu zera*, you have come to me to Paradise at the station, he is thinking. Arrived she had indeed, this Paz Mendi Elizagoyen resolved to fulfill her destiny; this Paz Mendi quite beside herself with fright. As the old buckaroo stood there dumbfounded and quite dazed, the young woman smiled with lips as voluptuous as they were innocent. She smiled he thought at him.

Par-a-dice? Is this Paradise? tentative shy, quite necessarily so, she asked the looming *fantasmada* of a man who stood there stiff as a flagpole.

Paradisoa ala? she asked him again, well aware of the charm that dimples brought to an otherwise overly serious face.

take me

But there was no answer. *E-che-varria-ra*? She took
her time with the familiar syllables thinking maybe
they, like she, had been born again. "Echevarria," how
ever else could it be? Little did she know, not only was
old Altube working up a lather, he was hard of hear-
ing and even harder of listening. The old cowman
had been twice struck by lightning to the head which
hadn't helped his vision none, nor his disposition. This
young filly miss-of-a-lass sure was out of his season,
but standing there penniless and regal before him—
she was perfect in her imperfection: Perfect for him, he
is thinking.

Truth was, Pedro Altube, caught with her out there
between quaken leaves and hoar frost, was not only
half-deaf and dying; at fifty-five winters, he was stone
cold alone. He fingered the stubble of a beard just beginning—took two steps back—and with a start,
looked down at his trousers—but it was too late. All
day at the stockyards, and now here at the station, Pedro de Altube realized he was fatefully smeared with
a greenly aromatic unguent: wooly lanolin mixed with
sheep shit and creek.

> *He had cattle and land beyond all wonder*
> *sheep too many to number*
> *but Pedro Altube had no sons . . .*

No remedio. He must give 'er a try. One never knows:
every chance could be a man's last grubstake.

(*Ona hemen nauzu, neska.*) Here you have me—your
Paradise, girl, he considered, but even he dared not say
this truth aloud.

Take me?

The late October light around them conspired pen-ultimate brilliance; the leaves fast swirling pockets of cruel golden hope had left them both enchanted. *Ankak gora* hooked upside down and drug by a stirrup in the last rodeo of his life, Altube now found himself play-ing the clown mounted on the ass of his own doddering ridiculousness. (Not in his wildest dreams had he ex-pected this). He knew he was a striking man (not hand-some but imposing). *He had cattle and land beyond all wonder/sheep too many to number* . . . He'd had women before—many women. Why, he was *el jinete del caballo blanco*, the straw boss of kings; but, at the moment, this near miss was riding roughshod all over him.

Hoh-tel Echevariuh? She asked again with an aspi-rate "*h*," a lay down "*r*," even a noncommittal Ameri-cano ending.

And still from him nothing. Why couldn't this cowboy answer her up front and decent? *Para-deese Ne-ba-da Ho-otel Echevarria A-mer-i-ka. Bien alors*, she practiced again in her head the spell to break the im-passe. Quite simply, the sun was at a slant and she knew she had to get along. Was this *Amerikanue* merely deaf and dumb, or blind as well to her standing out there on the street exposed to every María, Jesús y José?

It was then she first lost her patience. *Ezetz, mais non!* Who needed him? *Or konpon on se débrouillera* anyway. She would find this infernal Echevarria place herself. Turning on her heel, Paz Mendi headed in the opposite she-knew-not-to-where-direction; then, quite unaccountably, turned her head about deciding to indulge in one last tortuous glance up into that hat of his like a parasol which had almost sheltered both of them from the white Nevada sun. Paz Mendi was not unkind, she was not even inconsiderate: she was *bien élevée* and knew her manners well. One last interminable time only she would look up into that mad, quixotic face. Once more would she consider the comely crags of him carved out by high desert sands because he was her elder, because she knew better.

"Paradise, Nevada?" she asked this time in perfect English. Is this Paradise? Was it the words which were not registering with him, or was he put off by her odd foreignness—by her youth? Perhaps he couldn't hear the high tones of her voice? There was no telling with the elderly.

And as for him . . . *Bizarra!* The accursed word lingered in his head like a curse. *Bizarrrraaaa!* (He might have shaved.) *Txa-pe-la!* From the very beginning he knew he should have tipped the brim of his broad vaquero's hat in deference to a lady. If he removed it he knew the bald spot would appear. *D'Altube bai zera zu.* You so tall no one has ever seen the top of your head. (Perhaps that very fact had saved him up till now). *Baietz*, yes he was Pedro de Altube of the Spanish Ranch of the High Desert and she was no lady.

Take me

Out there on the spittle-stained boardwalk, out there like a ham hanging on public display, Pedro de Altube Idígoras stayed his ground because it was his ground. Although he'd been fast hobbled by her beauty (thoroughly shaken) Pedro de Altube was—Pedro Altube. As for her: she knew she soon must get away. As for him: he knew he could not go. He knew he could not stay.

By 3:17 the train had left the station. All the good folk had moseyed on, and still no response from the stranger who was getting stranger. *Egon zaitez* stay put there mister, she warned him with her eyes: eyes like the sun. Even though she'd resigned herself to her own indentured helplessness, Paz Mendi—just a poor foreign pilgrim—was mighty surprised when Monsieur Flagpole himself stayed planted. (With him, something must have registered.)

Goddamnittohell he knew she had him dead to rights, by the low-hangin *cojones* awright. *¿Que demonios?* What the hell was a man to say to a female anyway? (All these years and he still never knew.) What ever would they have in common? He, a "de Altube" and she, a more-common-than-commoner? Should he ask her about the month-long ocean voyage twice in estrus and in steerage? Ask about the thirty-one questions: *Could she read and write? Had she ever been in prison? Did she know anyone who was mentally insane?* At Ellis Island had she finally been disinfected? How about the train ride across a continent alone and with no common language? How did that all go?

Sonafoabeetches it was a cryin shame, this all too obvious disparity of generations. *Elle est bien dans sa peau*, and she fit her skin so well! This bumfuzzle predicament had put him in a dither. He couldn't remember the last time he had felt such fever. (Truth to tell, he couldn't really remember much of anything.) Don Pedro de Altube Idígoras de Oñati *zu zera* you are the one, but it is you you *zu*, Paz Mendi—your fresh beauty beyond all imagining—that is the sun.

Stillyet he was silent.

Mecauendiosgoddamittohellofasonofabeetches he cursed himself madly inside of his head all scrambled. He'd been shit-kicked to the curb, that much was certain. You think your time is up and the cattle drive over, the last sheep at night are bedded and all in, and then like a west wind—all cruel and delicious—time stirs you to living and dances you within.

But Paz Mendi wasn't cruel, not even hard-hearted: she was just dog-tired, and even though she had wisely limited her fluid intake as advised across the continent, Paz Mendi hadn't seen a toilet since Denver. Despite the agony, she took time to look down and consider his clownish long boots curling up at her smiling (no doubt special ordered) the left one worn clear through the toe. (*Gaizua*, poor fool.) Then she breathed not too deeply in consideration of her condition, and decided to start heading right down the street when—finally!- his answer. Or was it still a question?

Hemen duzu Paradisoa, andere. Here, your paradise, Lady, proclaimed the range-wracked voice to her as gift at last.

(My, my, "my lady," no less.) He was Basque!

Satisfied by his words, but put off by his manner, Paz Mendi turned on her heel and with a quick snap of her over-long neck like a swan (or was it a goose?) snatched up her satchel with steadfast determination in her stride. She would take herself to this infernal Basque hotel outpost!

At this critical juncture, a scroungy mongrel heading down the tracks due east toward Paradise darted between the two of them—Paz Mendi and Pedro Altube. The black dog veered north at the second corner in the direction of Chin's Cafe and Echevarria's Basque Hotel Saloon and Restaurante.

With the embers of the last fire in his groin lowly smouldering, Pedro Altube follows the girl who carries the bag who follows the dog two blocks up the street, all three of them finally headed in the right direction.

Take me.

Hemen duzu Paradisoa, andere. Here, your paradise, lady. Her death a sinkhole. This hole a mystery. No church bells in the New World portend her passing. No medieval steepled tintinnabulation. Today death sits at the table of Echevarria. *Ikusi nuanian/nik zure ahoa/ iruditu zitzaidan maitia/karobi zuloa.* The French bread is baking in the oven of your mouth.

Now, she is bound for America—to Paradise—her passage indentured making her free. In a white satin gown fashioned for a wedding in a hotel in a room on a table our lady is waiting, the cold baby pressed close to her breast. Out on the sea the rowers are rowing. Take Paz Mendi to Paradise. *Oh sister, sister take me, take me.*

Then they gathered round the knife-scored board and ate like princes: The table set with white linen, French crystal and Nevada silver. Come, come—*à table*, the funeral feast is readied—the fattened calf, the ruby wine. Today death eats at our table: 40 pounds of beefsteak, 13 pounds of lamb, 20 pounds of tripe, 4 pounds of bacon, 5 pounds of garbanzos, 6 pounds of navy beans, 26 bottles of wine; 17 loaves of bread, 15 chorizo sausages, 8 cans of peppers, 30 apples, 20 pears, 1 cinnamon stick, 1 bottle of vanilla, 1.5 pounds of sugar, 2 pints of cream, 2 pounds of coffee, 2 liters of brandy, 1 decanter of *pacharrán* . . . 1 box of cigars. A feast like no other for Paz Mendi. So many mourners there is no room.

As for him, *txa-la-par-ta ta* beat the rhy-thm beats him down like beejesus this ringing in his head. Down down into the ground beat beat beats out his life time beats his dispodic des ti ny. As the singers sing and the diners revel, at last hour *al último paso*, Pedro de Altube lord of the pampas, *vaquero de Méjico*—Spanish Ranch cacique and grandee, tips his hat and bids his lady "*Adieu.*"

Outside beyond the alleyway that separates Echevarria's Basque Hotel Saloon and Restaurante from Chin's Café there is a long dark passageway that opens from within. Two thousand horses can't keep him from the doorway. Forty thousand sheep and cattle can't keep him from entering. Even four-hundred-thousand acres can't keep him from his prison. The chains they are making him free.

Today nothing, not even death, stands in his way. Crossing the alley, then stooping low in the back doorway of Chin's Café, Pedro de Altube pegs the wide-brimmed sombrero of cacique and vaquero on the grapnel hook by the stairs where his great coat had been. By an underground light cast by whale oil and paraffin he finds the alcoved shelf sweated out by bodies reclining—the flat earthen platform made smooth by longing and by pain.

Gaiztozuloan now home alone on his own down in the caverns of his own beginning, Pedro Altube lifts the pipe that will bring sweet forgetting and rain. His seed now spent on the ground dead-wasted, Pedro Altube goes down in the tunnel dreaming of new worlds and sons, and dreaming of sons.

Eh meo Cid.

Document of Departure of Pedro Altube

Prepared in Oñate, Guipuzcoa 6 May 1845

. . . José Miguel de Altube, resident of this town, presented himself and declared that his brother Pedro de Altube, profession farmer, bachelor, native, and a resident of this town, with the blessings and approval of the declarant, lacking parents now deceased, has decided to embark and travel to the city of Buenos Aires in America, to join Don Santiago de Altube and two other brothers who reside in that locality. [The declarant desiring to guarantee the payment of the board and passage to Buenos Aires of the above stated young man, and noting that the ship Irurac Bat is readied to sail shortly form the port of Bilbao, said ship belonging to Espalza and Sons of the firm of that name, agrees to guarantee with his belongings and to transfer in payment to the stated firm Espalza and Sons, or their representatives, in cash, the amount or expenses of the board and passage of said young man Pedro de Altube. The payment of payments in the form agreed upon mutually will be made without delay or excuse, under pain of legal action and collecting costs in the event of default. [As an article of faith the declarant wherewith] mortgages specifically and expressly among his other family holdings, a portion of chestnut forest, with its land and trees, belongs to the declarant, and with a sale's value of three thousand reales vellon, situated in the district called Escorta erreca, barrio Zubillaga, in this municipality, and bordered on one side by the chestnut forest of the farmsteads Urteaga-garaicoa and Antuenga, and on the other by that of the farmstead Aspicoa.

Archivo de la Universidad de Oñate, Legajo 3610

LA HISTORIA DE LOS BASCONGADOS EN EL OESTE DE LOS ESTADOS UNIDOS, SOL SILEN, 1917

There is clear evidence of Basque personalities in the cattle industry of the Great Basin by 1871. It was in that year that two established Basque cattlemen of California Pedro and Bernardo Altube began ranching operations in Independence Valley (Elko County, Nevada), close to the mining town of Tuscarora. By the time they were in their early forties Pedro and Bernardo Altube occupied positions of wealth, prominence, and respect among California Basques. We have already considered some of their business dealings. According to one account, however, the Altubes felt the pressures of increased crowding on the California ranges and purchased 3,000 head of cattle in Mexico, trailing them to Independence Valley, where they established the huge "Spanish Ranch". When dissolved in 1907, the sale included 400,000 acres, 20,000 head of cattle, 20,000 sheep, and 2,000 horses.

1912
Anastacia
Echevarria

Etchek' an-dere handi
ninduzun eguerdi gainian,
Alhargun gazte gelditu nintzen
iguzkia sarthu senian.

At noon I was
the lady of the house
by sunset a widow alone.

Today. The kitchen was dim. The moon had slipped
out dissipate from behind dark clouds. Night devoured
day. The chairs were emptied. The stove gone cold. The
clock on the wall had stopped. Now she was all alone.
Bakar-bakarrik. Whose woman was she?

Together, Ana Madariaga and Elias Echevarria
had stacked hours into days
into months into years like
cords of stovewood on the
back porch of this godfor-
saken frontier outpost they

Maria WIFE OF
Eladio AGUIRRE
Aug. 24, 1894
Jan. 22, 1926

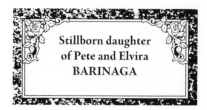

Stillborn daughter
of Pete and Elvira
BARINAGA

dared call a "sheep ranch." Together they had buried their babies—her mother, then her father; an uncle from Lequetio, an unidentified neighbor, their loyal sheepdogs, cats and some kittens, a bird and a young cousin barely arrived—had buried them here in this ground.

Yesterday, he had wound the clock before leaving (his habit always after breakfast). Yesterday, the legs of his chair had scraped the wooden floor. Yesterday, she had watched him rub his bum knee sitting next

Peter Ramon
Son of Ramon
and
Grace Lugea
1910–1925

the cookstove, watched him set the Stetson square on his head after he had shrugged broad shoulders deep into the sheepskin coat that had once been her father's. *Begi-begiz*, furtive yet intensely, she had watched him hoping this time, once just once, he would turn to lighten her load, and acknowledge her pain. She needed him to hold her in the black pit of their fast losses together, but he always turned his own way away. Yesterday, she remembered. He had cleared the walk of snow with the flat shovel, walked back to return it to the back porch, then let the screen door slam shut behind him on the wooden frame (as was his custom). He never turned back again.

> *Amaiera asiera da*
> Ashes to ashes dust to dust
> *Tuntunturrun tun*
> I am Ramon.

The beginning is always the end ... this beginning. *Gaur*, today after preparing the mid-day meal, she would sit in his chair next the woodstove for morning prayers, for the counting of her blessings. Dressed only in a nightshift, she bent down to the mouth of the stove, coaxed fire from the coals as her body swooned, faltered, her legs spindley those of a newborn calf. She would sit in his chair next to the woodstove. Repeat. Repeat familiar motions. Again again the living motions. Prod, jab, shift the embers. Prod, jab, turn. Bring him to life again again make him red

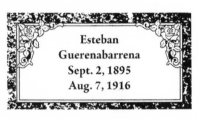

Esteban
Guerenabarrena
Sept. 2, 1895
Aug. 7, 1916

glowing. Bring him up, bring him up from the grave, her milk overflowing! Put it on the stove to se-par-ate the rich cream *kipura* cream. The rich skin of fat floats skim skim it was for his breakfast. She would sit in his chair next the woodstove for morning prayers, for the counting of her blessings. *Suscipe.*

She saw his face now still alive—an odd expression. *Elias* whisper tender she kissed him. Closed the lids of each eye, tasting each corner's sweet salt. The drifts outside stood high stood frozen. The ice solid beneath the weight of heavy snowfalls, the sheep were trapped within. After stopping the clock, she set the two Carson City dollars down heavy upon his lids. She folded his

Francisco Goicoechea
Murió
MAY 18 1914
A LOS 32 AÑOS

hands neatly one upon another as her mother, grandmother before her had done. All her life came now *auxe* only to this? His life, this long body wrapped stiff? This frozen shape thawing too quickly *isharraz sepultarean* this this covered by a funerary cloth, her husband? It was a full day before they had found him buried by the blizzard. If not for the dog, it might not have been till spring.

The men had taken great pains not to break him, finally laying him straight out, fast-frozen in the wagon. Once at the ranchhouse they carried him to her, carried him in quickly as if there were some hurry. Carried him like some frontier Jesus, then set him atop their marriage bed there being no other bed. There, she had spent the vigil *argitzailetan* stoking the fire all the night long watching him—to her horror—gradually thaw. The closest priest was a two days' journey. *Auzokoak,* the nearest neighbors some twenty miles distant, had stayed holed up on their places waiting out the storm. The men inside the house were restless, were hungry. She hoped and prayed she had not yet become someone's quick opportunity. Let sleeping dogs lie. *Agur Ma ri a Graa zi aas Hail Mary Mother of Grace* now and at the hour of our death. Now whose woman was she?

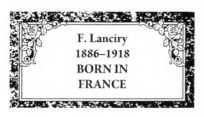

F. Lanciry
1886–1918
BORN IN
FRANCE

She is aware of things, as if from under water: the echo of time in incessant slow running. Feels numbly her fingers cut pieces of red cubed potatoes; carrots phallic tapered and lean. She peels and chops the onions and garlic adding chunks of spring lamb to the pot. Beneath the window in the garden below her the pickaxe pierced, gored whole open the tough skin

Tomas Zuazola
1894–1918

of the earth. Spear-like, the metal sang as it split the
roots subterranean blue broken into so many spidery
veins. The ring, ring, ring of their shovels hit the crust
of the earth sure tolling sounding the knell of the funeral dirge. But for all their exertion, for all their hard
labor, only the topsoil was loosened: the underearth lay
hard frozen till early May below. Watching them from
the window in the withining moments slow falling she
couldn't remember where he had gone, who he had
been. Whose woman was she?

*The day has fled. She is weeping for she has lost her
only child who was the light of her life. Suddenly a
weird light, mysterious. Child of my heart, are you
happy?* Arguiduna etorri da. *The One of Light has
come, the dead in the light of her eyes Mother Spirit
Mother Earth Andra Mari Mother of Love shifting
shape, warns of danger. The bluish-white light ac-
companies the spirit vessel as Antonio and Gabriela
approach the water fountain to drink deep of the
philter knowing after quenching their thirst they
will have no control over themselves, no control in
this world. Warn them! Comfort them!* Arguiduna
dana daki. *Arguiduna knows your loss.* Arguiduna zuretzat negar egiten. *Arguiduna weeps alone
for you. Aiiieeeeeee . . .*

The wind screams within the dream. For a moment
she holds the tiny hand in hers beneath the frozen soil.
For a moment only, marvels at the miracle of just-
formed fingernails shelled like raindrop pearls of beginning. "Those are pearls that were his eyes," says she.

*It is the left hand of a child severed during sleep
and wrapped with curls of its own hair that is the*

> *amulet to deliver one from danger. Philters could*
> *be made from the fresh blood of children in a hot*
> *soup that could invigorate the weakened bodies of*
> *women especially after childbirth, sometimes sav-*
> *ing their lives (the witch* sorgin *had told her.* "Ez
> geala, ba geala." *We all are to be not to be.*

She turns from the window to the stove and stokes
the fire again with the iron poker. The stake struck se-
par-ate, they said. The right arm pulled off like a twig
 along with the machinery.
The rib cage was cracked
opened like a walnut
comme ça zast. She bastes
the mutton fast in its own
juices, tills the carrots, on-
ions and potatoes again about the roasting meat thinking he would be hungry again. Since morning *café esne
ogia'ko koskorraz bakarrik* he still hadn't eaten the
midday meal that would sustain him through the long
day. She bathes the body anointing his lifeless flesh,
caresses the separate folds of skin: each muscle, each
bone she herbs with the unguent of precious aromatic oil Gregoria had brought. There being no priest, she
takes out the vial reserved deep within the cedar chest,
reserved only for birth and for death. Many times
throughout the long watch she holds out the long
arms—one and then another—imaging them round
her waist, holds the familiar rough hands, callused by
hard labor in her own hands, each one a relic of flesh,
of bone, smooths finally the muscled limbs separate
and oiling, cleanses the fingers and toes one by one
until he is ready. Her sadness is she will cook for him
no more. *Nere maitea, nik zuretzatopilla surtan daukat,*

Peter
Son of
Mr & Mrs
Guy Aguirre

My darling, I have for you a lovely cake. *Erdi-erdiya emango dizut beste erdiya neretzat,* I shall give you half, the other half for me.

Outside. The men have finished their attempt at digging: Beltran, Antonio, Mateo Txiki had come as extra hands for the inopportune lambing and found a worse disaster—a man's death in the blizzarded storm. They stir awkwardly outside now, shy and ravenous, slink and linger like timber wolves beneath her window waiting. *Zer egin?* What should they do? None of them up to talking to a woman, none of them well prepared. The sun is going down. Dinner is ready. Death sits at our table today. Despite their considerable exertion, they cannot dig a trench for the body in the cold frozen ground. It is twenty below and holding. Time to give up the ghost now, time for coming in. The man was probably better off left frozen. *Who would bring him in?*

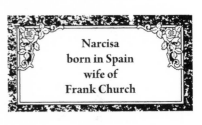

Narcisa
born in Spain
wife of
Frank Church

Inside, their meal is readied: the mutton rare yet, a deep pink roast of flesh left in the oven redolent of onions, of garlic. The men eat silent grateful, overcome by the hunched back of the woman at the sink. In time, the wine warms them one by one as they begin to talk in an improvised encomium to the man Elias Echevarria who just yesterday with them had lived. The bones and limbs, the heart and brain of the body they had attempted to plant shallow in the ground became their tribute: a frozen

GOICOECHEA
baby girl
1912

tribute to hard work and pain. The minutes stretched like sleeping cats, swelled languorous lengthened life out distancing the clock that had stopped to the sound of the glasses now clinking. At last they relaxing, their faces beginning to flush in the living with the wine, the life-giving meat. The woman turned away from them dumbly observing her reflection stupidly in the bubble-paned glass. Covertly now she watches their eyes lit by the glowing butts of cigarettes oxygenated by lungs through the fat funnels they fashion from the tubes of their lips. *Whose woman was she? Where did he end and she begin?*

At last, the veil of night came upon them all. The darkness a comfort, the darkness a shroud. She turned up the oil lamps and set the plates in the sink to soak. She stoked the fire again and put the old tin kettle on to boil as the window panes melted before her and hot glass poured

Son of Julian
& Marie Jayo
April 3, 1932

molten down the cold walls. She, Ana, poor desperate swimmer, struggled against the current, thrashed herself endless against the tide of the doorways, felt the vortex swirl about her forever vertiginous tentacled everywhere whirling. After they had gone, she collapsed down alone upon the floor deep in her own trench dug black of silent hyacinths, her brain blue-purple mottled so deep she was birthing, she was spreading. Frantic, her mind held on, last desperate she clutched a piece of gray driftwood, her body thrown up at once upon some distant shore.

She would keep the body fast frozen on the back porch. When the blizzard cleared, take him in the buckboard on the stage road to Echevarria's. Whose woman was she? *Who was she now without him?*

The mounds above her, the sky below. Her babes, their faces—Bernat, Ana: their fresh faces eaten by worms, their baby bodies shut tight in home-fashioned boxes left cold in the ground under the snow. *Elias Elias Elí* exiled, left now in a sheep shed, lost to her forever. All she had left, the frozen garden. Their little stones. *Bonbolontena, nere laztana.* Darling lambkin, My precious heart, *Aizteritxuak eramango zaitut erbiya zeralakuan. Bo!* The vulture will snatch you quick like a rabbit! Boo! Lullaby. *Aie Ama!* Her hand frozen groped, reaching deep down through the snow down *heriotzaraiño* to death. She reached into the islands of earth there, fingered small tender bulbs deep nuggeted beneath them: hyacinths fall-seeded purple in bloom first flower hyacinths what was their name in Basque then? Did they have an identity in the Old World? Hyacinths! Her father's favorite, poked finger-like first through the earth out the snow: together they had planted them in the garden last year, together last year dreaming of spring. Beneath the mound she clutched the baby limbs frozen underground, held them soft fresh inert. She felt again her husband's hand beneath the cold linen sheet. His lean body stirred moving restless within her. As she turned to kiss him, his eyes rolled out of his head in a nightmare became bulbs in the mingling in a deep purple tangle of roots. His body left her body. The tissues flush with fluid watered the underearth of her—blood, salt water, semen. The bones and kidneys, heart and collarbone; skull, whiskers, toenails and flesh of the man now lay transfigured beneath the mound of snow grew miraculous into worms and roots, moles and carrots, became the sleeping hyacinths of spring.

Yesterday, Ana rose at dawn from the narrow bed before him as was her custom. She threw on the old woolen wrapper, happily shuffling into the kitchen, the soft soles of his over-large slippers warming her feet. She smiled to herself softly singing *Agur Mar-ri-a graziaz betea zurekin* with you Mother. They still had time. They were young enough yet: there was hope. Deftly with the motion born of many mornings, she stacked again the kindling architected up leaving hidden a trellis from beneath which the fire could resuscitate, breathe. *Nere aurra lotxo, lotxo* sleep, my child, sleep/*Nik emanen dizkizut* I will give you *bi kokotxo* two sweets too sweet to eat.

Tun, kurrun, kurrun, kutun, kutun . . .

Daylight came and the secret stayed in the kitchen within her, a miracle held high between dark and lightness nestled in the roots of her womb. As Elias slept on in their bed she ground coffee, skimmed the thick, yellow cream from the milk and took out the basket of eggs saved for his breakfast. She cut across the bread drawing with the knife deftly a cross the rounded loaf and then sliced it again into the hunks with which he loved to dip dip into the wide bowl of sugared milk steaming. *Andra Mari Ana* he had whispered into her neck. She was happy, softly singing. If it were a boy she would call him "Lias." A girl, "Elia" after him.

Elias took his place in his chair next to the woodstove. He hooked the heels of his boots on the lower rung worn slick by the years, and coughing, looked down at the patched knees of his work trousers. The snow drifts stood high, solid still about the lambing sheds. She watched him nervous covert as his glance shifted out at once to the frozen fields beyond the window. Ana handed him his coffee secret smiling as he stuck his long nose deep into the heavy porcelain mug and warmed his hands about its base. Her man ate in silence tearing great chunks crumbling of sheepherder's bread from the loaf. He fretted fidgeting with his belt buckle getting ready to take his leave. Nevada *elurretan*, the snow drifts were heavy and high: the Rubies loomed snow purple in the distance. The sheep were all in, but a vicious storm threatened baring its teeth beyond the windows. His glance then darted intermittently out to the sheds and the barn. She knew she held him only with her body and the food, by dawn he would always seek the lone lean spell of the mountains again. *Goiko mendian elurra dago/errekaldean izotza* high, high in the mountains snow/in the lowlands on the river ice ice. She knew, come morning, his eyes would turn from her, lost in his own true purpose on earth he would leave. *Bijar datorenean* when tomorrow ever comes.

   In the doorway the man turned his eyes away from her gaze. She sensed his muscles turn taut stretch across the shoulders readying for day. As the seconds of the clock ticked away Ana felt him slip from her, sucked sudden far into the distance: a high desert argonaut catching the sole orbit of his own earth. She went out to the pantry, chose one jeweled jar of her autumn labor from the rubies, ambers and emeralds. Set it down as an offering before him on the table as he wiped his whiskers with a cloth napkin absently rubbing his slow morning knee in a circular caress of readiness. *Ez jun*, don't go out in the storm! *Jan behar dun. Lan egin behar dut*, his only reply. If you must eat, then I must work. And at that he laughed! *Those are pearls that were his eyes.*

She turned back towards the stove, opened the heavy iron door and raked the fire with a long poker he had fashioned for her on the forge. She thought ahead to the midday meal *bazkaria*. There were extra hands because of a too early lambing. Maybe they would become snowbound: she must plan ahead. The sky snarled warningly gray in the clouded March morning. She rearranged the pile of laundry dividing it by kind, checked for stains, then chose what she would soak from the rest. She drew up all the underclothes into a pile set aside and abruptly—too abruptly—his chair scraped the floor: wood against tile. *Gaur egun egon* stay just today stay stay. Absently, she watched her husband as he set the Stetson on his head, shrugged his shoulders deep into sheepskin, went out the back door. He cleared the walk of snow for her, returned the shovel to the back porch and turning again walked away without ever looking back.

Inside, the kitchen went chill. She went to stoke the fire again. In the darkness he moved toward her lowly in practiced movements. Tender, she smoothed the taut skin baked walnut by the summers of bare-chested labor. The fingers of her mind stretched alive and awakened reviving the still warm desire as she touched him. Within the singing of her memory she lingered, tracing again his live miracle of body: hair-studded elastic drape of skin stretched drum-like tight perfect across the collarbone, shoulders and ribs. The fine contours of sinew and muscle curve stretching in him, then relaxing and loosening as he moved ocean-like above her before leaving her hand. His skull, the hard lengths of his bones. *Nere gixon,* my man.

She lifted the undershirt, moist up off the chair, shook out the still warm scent of him. She breathed in

the male smell of sweat, soil and tobacco where it settled now about her dissipate beneath her touch. Then
she took the garment out to the soapy tub, began rhythmically scrubbing as she prayed while finishing. *Eman
ezazu gaur/Gure gaurko ogia* Give us this day/Our daily
bread. She rubbed the cloth briskly up and down and
back across evenly rhythmed against the washboard
ridged against her bent fingers. Almost finishing, the
square cake of lye soap inflamed her skin leaving a rash
on her hands red and raw. Before checking the pot of
beans, she rinsed his undershirt wringing the cloth in
tight cylindrical whorls and hung it up to dry on the
corded line above the stove. *Bijarko bear.* He would
need it. Tomorrow.

> I kept my husband's corpse with me
> seven years at home,
> By day in the cold ground,
> at night in my arms.
> *Con agua de naranjas le lavaba,*
> *una vez por semana, la mañana de los viernes*
> With orange water I bathed him
> bathed him once a week
> every Friday morning.

1922

"Gabriela had risen from her couch; smiling and blushing, she sought the oaken seat which was placed at the window. Seated on that ancient bench, she had listened to the first declaration of love, and there also had she avowed what she felt. Gabriela was beautiful. Each day the first rays of the aurora had been reflected in her lovely eyes. The first gentle breezes of morning had joyfully hastened to play among the chestnut tresses of the maid of Guipuzcoa. The very flowers bent their supple stems and the maiden passed, as though the lily, the daisy and the purple iris were saluting her the queen of the flowers. The graceful damsel, after waiting seated for the coming of her lover for a considerable time, at last bent her head and leaned out of her window to listen with attentive ear to the noises of the night."
—*Legends and Popular Tales of the Basque People*

He stared stupidly down at the hem of the pongee frock at her dimpled knees bedazzled by its creamy peachness. She was standing in the alley now, a kewpie doll vision topped by a glossy black flapper bob—all Clara Bow and vamp-in-waiting: beautiful child. Standing there before her, the China boy was deeply ashamed of his own poor coolie pants and the dusty canvas shoes. He himself could not bear the totality of his half-starved gawkiness. How must *he* appear to *her?* From their first tragic moment breathing together Lee loved Leonora: She was perfect, but who was he?

You talk funny quick E-Lee. You look funny too, your eyes are all squinty. You have no lids!

I . . . talk . . . quick quick . . . for you, he said so carefully he thought his heart would break before he could manage to articulate the hard consonants of the non-French Know Nothing tongue. (*For you you you, visage de porcelaine.*)

Strange boy. What are you? Aren't you *Basque?* she asked with all the incredulity of the pampered pet who is of her own world only.

I am. Chi-nois, he replied confusing the two languages which tumbled about all foreign in his head.

That's not a thing to be Elias E-Lee, the princess replied stomping out his green hope with her perfectly dainty foot.

After their brief conversation the boy managed to maintain his tottering position as the girl continued staring into the exotic wonder of him. Lee began to wonder why he was alive. Cruel, wistful star of his engendering. Who had been his father? Why did his life matter? (To her it didn't). In short, why was Lee, *he?*

What he wanted wasn't she, it was words words words to tell her of this feeling in his chest—to explain the moveable feast within him. There simply was no language for it: neither Basque nor English, not even Chinese. For him still standing there, this moment was nothing short of an Inquisition of exquisite torture. Her skin, *porcelaine.* Her eyes, indescribable. She, the cream dream of a moon he would never touch.

What he did not know was that the pure animal grace of him had charmed her completely—his cat slant eyes, his chamois skin. He was perfect in his imperfection, this strange China boy, this "Lee." Despite the untoward fact of his pedigree, the problem of his eyes and skin for grown-ups (Who ever understood *them?*), Leonora recognized nothing but his solidity, the resiliency of him. He would not speak directly to her, just in a faltering off way aside. No matter. Leonora knew at once he was her protector and champion. For her he would be be knighted, E-Lee Elias Eli.

There were no words no words and he was no-thing, the Know Nothings said. He was Lee (*no remedio*) there was no remedy for a thing such as he. Quite tragically she was Leonora: she was his princess—her tiger eyes wind in dry grass.

Knowing tinder kindles quickly, she lit it anyway and he agreed to burn.

Pedro Echevarria and Gregoria Malasechevarria had one hotel, a bar and restaurant; a house in town with an English garden on Court Street, and at any given time two to four bands of sheep, a haberdashery, half interest in the Gaiety Theater, a French-Chinese laundry; seven daughters (Amelia, Grace,

Marie, Elena, Honorina—who had died as an infant—
Lucretia, Leonora) and one only son—Peter Ramon—
taken quite quickly at twelve by the Spanish flu.

By 1922 the prospects of Pedro, resident *hotelero*
and man-about-town, had paid off for the denizens
of Echevarria's Basque Hotel Saloon and Restaurante: even the mining claims were turning up pay dirt.
Admittedly, some business arrangements had gone
decidedly south with the changes after the Great War,
and there was still Prohibition (never an innkeeper's
dream), but over all Peto had hedged his bets enough
for all major stakes in Paradise to know fruition.

Bustling and buxom, Gregoria Echevarria was
a formidable woman of some substance: a queen in
her own dominion whom her husband Pedro called
"heifer-hipped" with no faint affection. His wife
was simply and appropriately called Goya by most of
Paradise. She held her throne as reigning kitchen god-
dess and reverend mother to the hangdog and orphaned
of Echevarrria's; but this Mari Red Queen, *como una
fiera,* was all too often overcome by the hair trigger of
her own estuarine temper. There were no small number of citizens of Paradise who had become the fast
victims of her verbal pyrotenics. *Zelako txupinakoak!*
Word around town was that Gori could "*gorritu,*" heat
up real quickly, then like a mad shepherdess with a
sheephook take you out at the knees. (It would all be
over before you knew it.)

The fireworks of Mrs. Echevarria were such a con-
trast to the earthy warm home of her that no one in
Paradise ever knew quite what to think. Everyone who
was anybody knew full well that Don Pedro, was a no-
torious and careless (for that you couldn't forgive him)
philanderer and man-about-the-wrong-side-of-the-

tracks-around-town. As a result, the connubial lives of Pedro and Gregoria Echevarria had been an unending series of pregnancies and miscarriages. In twenty years of marriage, Goya's reproductive engine had fired at least ten times, produced two full-term fetuses, lost a baby daughter, and her one and only son. By 1922 the marital relations "Echevarria" had become considerably strained.

> The Free Press, Feb 23, 1922
>
> The Overland Hotel is the proud possessor of one of the latest type of orchestral equipment. It is valued at $2,500 contains 17 instruments and, when played resembles the great pipe organs in million dollar theaters. The new music producer is finding much favor among the hotel's patrons. When the nickel is dropped in the slot, one can close his eyes and imagine himself in a theater in San Francisco, listening to one of the pipe organ artists at a well-known playhouse in the bay city.

If Pedro Echevarria was the Great Provider of Paradise, Gregoria was Earth Mother Birther, Chief Cook and Bottle Washer. As for him, few men blamed Pedro his indiscretions. As for her, there was not a woman who could abide him, with the exception of those who did. Echevarria's Basque Hotel Saloon and Restaurante was a critical frontier outpost in Paradise: On final accounts, usually no one really blamed either of them.

For now, Pedro (whom his wife Goya called "Peto" with no faint affection) took solace in the storehouse basement of his fine Basque-American hotel. Underground—his refuge, his *confort*: he knew the beneath earth like a ground squirrel knows the intricate contours of its own cool-walled lair. Down here, where Peto stood tall for a shortish man, he was lord and master of all he surveyed. Above, there was always the echo and clatter of fast, busied voices: his wife Goya at central command; but down below, his precious entrepôt hid stockpiles of supplies inventoried at his very fingertips. In the cellars of Echevarria, down in this basement cool, the open veins of spilled wine rivered along the packed earthen floor drying to maroon; the Serrano-style hams rubbed red fragrant raw there all rock salt and paprika awaiting; the bulging red *chorixoak* sausages hung pendulant and ready from festooned strings. *Le grand hôtelier* surveyed his dispensations like a minor cacique. There were two things to comfort him only (besides fishing): for now, there was going under; sometime later, going *out*.

One thing was certain about her hips: Gregoria Echevarria had always stood squarely established upon them. Even she admitted, with each child came another ten pounds and with each pregnancy (of which there had been ten) she noticed the compass needle of her husband's eye straying farther west, farther east. It roamed the hotel and the board-walked streets of Paradise. It roamed the bars and gambling joints and finally its gaze came to rest upon the red line of flash lit houses along the railroad tracks bringing to Goya a new private grief. In the end, truth be told, the red lit houses on the other side would leave the lady of the house of Echevarria's alone with a loneliness that the bustling hotel and her family could never fill. *Bizi il arte.* Live until you die. What else? *¿Qué remedio?*

Man dies, his white bones are dumb without a word when the green pines feel the coming of the spring. Li Po

---

Virginia City Chronicle, December 7, 1878

Won Look, a Tartar of high standing and a member of the Masonic fraternity died after a prolonged illness. He requested that his obsequies should be conducted on the American plan.

Elko Free Press, February 8, 1912

We notice the Chinese flag is floating from the mast-head on the Consul House and also in front of the Joss House. We are informed by Hi Loy the big day comes off next Wednesday. Delegates are expected from Carlin, Palisade and other neighboring places to assist in the celebration. General preparations are now going on at the Joss House by the Chinese celebrants. Hi Loy extends to his white friends a cordial invitation to witness the ceremony and listen to the events inside of the Chinese To-Tom.

Eh, Maritixu, Nora zoaz? Where you goin? We got the
wedding reception in two hours *jentille ba-dira* import-
ant people, Goicoechea *bakizu*, you know.
   Internura.
   To a funeral?! Whose funeral?
   The funeral of Tiny Lee.
   The Chinaman?
   Bai-zera. Jun bear. I must go.
   But he's a Chinaman!
   Auzurrikourrena. He is neighbored kin.
   Ze demonioak, emaztea? What the hell, wife?
   Kandelak emon bear. We are attending neighbors.
   Ezetz, hembra! I forbid you to do this, female!"
As Goya slammed shut the screen door of the ho-
tel's front door, her husband, Pedro Echevarria, *etxe-
jaun* (their lord and master) returned to his coffee. He
could quite happily sit down now in his chair, read the
morning paper completely undisturbed.

   Ni hao. (Did I say it right, Lee?)
   Pinjian zhi jiao bu ke wang Meez Echeverri.
   What does he say, my son?
   A friendship forged in hardship is never for-
gotten.
   Hil eta gero, oilo salda.
   What does she say, Xuiming? =
   Chicken soup for whatever ails you.
   Ha yes yes! Very good advice. Yes. What else
she say?
   *Gizon bizar pituti, eta emazte bizarzuti,
Iges-egik.*
   What mean then, boy?
   Run from the man without a beard and the
woman with one!

Beranduegi, too late—the strange girl had spoken: the one with yellow coyote eyes. "Run, run from the woman with one! Ha! Haha ha. *Zer Amaa? Miña egiten nau.* Aie Ama! you're hurting me, Mother! Beware of the man without a beard. The woman with one! Ha!" And they laughed together so heartily the three of them: Goya, Lee Ah Lake and Lee, that the small Indian funeral band stopped for a moment their cymbaled racket and turned pausing at the Nevada Bank of Commerce. (The Chinese never seemed to mind that the only musical ensemble available for such an event was Paiute or Shoshone since their rhythmically odd squawk and flat drumming served as adequate protection against the wrath of the underworld, not to mention displeased ancestors.)

It was a dusty procession in the midday sun of at least twenty Chinese bearing red wax candles and oddly squared flags moving from the Chinese gardens on the south side of the tracks north toward the city dump up Fifth Street. The clamoring funeral parade went past the Joss House, then by the two-story red Tong building, continued past Echevarria's Basque Hotel Saloon and Restaurante making its ultimate way on up towards the white man's graveyard on the hill.

Wing Lee, uncle of Tiny Sing and grandfather to Tommy Long, had been prominent in the Chinese community of Paradise despite the fact that in Caucasian eyes he was a lowly vegetable farmer; nevertheless, he was the undisputed source of most of the fresh produce in Paradise: onions, potatoes, carrots, green beans, lettuces, radishes, Chinese cucumbers, turnips, celery and the grown-to-order harvest for Echevarria's: garlic, leaks, precious red peppers, even exotic white asparagus. Apart from the hot house tomatoes that Goya cultivated throughout the year in the high parlor sun-room of the hotel, Wing Lee and his garden were a ver-itable life source to Echevarria's.

The bells oddly chiming out of place on the West-ern street, the bright flag-like banners, the cymbal and other improvised instruments of the Great Paiute Chi-nese Funeral Cortege Band were certain to ward off all evil spirits: Chinese, Paiute, Basque and otherwise. Up the downtown, down the uptown all together moving west: one stout Basque matron with blue eyes like a spring sky, one tall half-breed Chinese boy fast turn-ing into a man, one spoiled coquette of a six year old girl (who certainly knew her worth) and the remaining members of the Chinese Free Mason Benevolent Soci-ety Tong of Paradise, Nevada.

Arimak al dogu hembrak, Ama? Do women have souls, Mother? asked the child innocently.

Zer diozu ba? What's that you say?

Souls. Lee says the Chinese doubt it. Do we?

Kasuz, umetxo. Probably, child.

This new world, Silver Mountain, was incomprehensi-ble to him. How had it all come to be? Wasn't it the Chinese whose labor had brought the railroads? The Chinese who mined the gold? Chinese, who swept and washed and cooked and cleaned? The Chinese who had brought water to Paradise and Tuscarora with their ca-nals. Chinese who tilled the soil bringing forth the veg-etables, the flowers for their town gardens. The source of everything in Paradise it seemed to Lee was the Chi-nese! How then did the white devils call them "guests"? How the Know Nothings blind and deaf in their great-ness pass him on the street with no acknowledgment?

Was this Gold Mountain? Silver? Land of all riches?
Land of the free? How was he Lee? No thing at all.

As children Elora and Lee were fast sealed within her
grandiose ego and his love. Sometimes in the darkness they scratched the ground beneath the town of
Paradise digging in the Chinese tunnels with their
mouths, moving forward with their claws. Some old
men still spoke of the secret digging of the dens. The
Know Nothings hadn't even known until the tunnels
had been completed and some of theirs had descended to the opium dens, had paid to stay the soft, hazy
while on the short earthen shelves. Some had even said
old Wang had discovered a vein of gold beneath the
town digging the tunnels but went to his grave with
the knowledge of its exact location. Others said it was a
pipe dream of wishful thinking. Half a century later, it
would be Lee himself who would wonder if the tunnels
had really ever been there. Lee who would think: If the
Mother Lode were really in deep veins hidden beneath
the town, would the citizens of Paradise sacrifice their
here and now for a golden hereafter?

For now, as children *itzaleetan* in the shadows underground, the Chinese tunnels of moist gloom and forgetting belonged to them alone; beneath the streets of
Paradise they had access to the vast underground: The
Nevada Hotel, The Depot, The Palm Saloon, J. C. Ste-
vens, The Silver Dollar, Anacabe's, The Paradise Barber
Shop, the Gaiety Theater! Sometimes they even heard
voices, listened to them at the secret portals of each
place. Indians at The Palace Bar! Pistoleroak at Roop's
Pool Hall! exclaimed Leonora. Hush or they'll hear
us, whispered Lee. One time when Old Lung wasn't

watching the door of the laundry and had left it open, they heard a liquor-tongued woman and a man—Aita! Leonora was shocked to hear her father's voice. And most shocking of all: Americans with Chinese! Something to do with counting, with gold and a fast deal between them. In the poker games they could hear Doc Gallagher, Judge Tabor, and the fat man who wheezed, the president of the Nevada Bank of Commerce. *What was his name?*

Still, yet still in the recesses of cool earth they pressed their sweet sweating child bodies together and listened deeply to the words they could catch muffled by at least a foot or two of packed dirt. *Leizaetan* in the caves of Mari in Spain, Ama had told them lived Mari with Basajaun lord of the forest. Pressed in their own cave togethered their flesh as one, you could hear the breathing of the boy, the girl's sweet open-mouthed soughing. There was no other language between them. It was so cool underground in the hot summertime, sometimes they'd even sleep.

Gaur jai eguna! Today, Tía Ana's wedding at Echevarria's. Today there would be shrimps and leg of lamb, *des profiteroles, des gâteaux Basques.* She knew they would be so preoccupied there would be no retribution for her plan. *¡Coqueta!* little flirt darling, would be Aita's perennial exclamation when he saw her carmine sheath fashioned of the finest silk sewn by Long the Chinese tailor who had (just for her) embroidered delicate white peonies crafted from fine Chinese thread. *In golden sunshine her rosy robe is dyed/My silkworms are hungry, I cannot stay!*

As the last word on children in the house of Echevarria, the girl knew the sun rose and never set with her. She was Leonora, the last child of Peto and Goya's middle age: too precious to question. *Gaur egun*, today was a day she would be beautiful for everyone (she felt generous), but first she had to hatch her plan. If they asked her she would cast down those gold tinged eyes, then turn them upward head turned sideways again. That would get them! How could they admonish her? Today was *ezkontz-eguna* a wedding day; her cousin Eliana was coming and soon it would be her birthday too! Today, the Echevarria girls would wear fine silk dresses from Paris, an English worsted gentlemen's suit for Pedro the dandified *pater familias*. Today, the progeny of Echevarria's would don six exquisite gold wristwatches purchased to grace the family photo to send to family *etxekoak* in Spain, to whom their American successes must be made manifest. Completing the perfect picture was Aita with his gold pocket watch; Ama with a timepiece diamonded like a constellation of maternal time hanging pinned from a solid gold chain upon her still somewhat Edwardian-styled breast. Yes yes *baietz*.

Leonora was typically up in the birdhouse aviary beneath a ceiling of glass. Aita had had John Perry from the railroad bring the birds to entertain her as chicks from San Francisco. She knew their voices so well as they fussed, twittered and cackled. Now she recalled that first time setting them free she had opened the gilded cage and they had gone wild-joyed in a new abandon that had terrified her. Colors swirled about the room, all flapping wings and delicious squawks. *Cucuru cu cúú! Ka aka Kiri . . . kiri couuoooocoo!* The cockatiels, parakeets and canaries were all singing for her now dressed up in their Sunday yellow blues. Lovely all a twitter, their hatch-marked stripes their high happied chirping then sudden warning. *Ttssssst! Lara lara lara la la la . . . Bainan honela/Ez zen geihago/Txoria izango. If I clipped her wings/She would be mine/But then she would no longer be a bird.*

Ama said it was *tontuen bearra*, fool's labor to set them free when all they knew was a cage: cruel somehow. *Gogoak ixildu bear* one must quiet their longings, their desires as they themselves were kept: domesticated birds, a race genetically designed to not reach for the sky. *Txori-Nori-a*, Goya's pet name for the overprecious eighth child and seventh daughter of Echevarria. On too many an occasion left to her own devices, in the end there had been no dinner. Far too often, Ama had slapped her bottom . . . hard! It stung, but it had always been worth the price to exercise her own overarching autonomy. Strange that the worst whipping had come from letting the birds all go. Why would giving the joy of freedom ever be wrong? Leonora herself was deeply chagrined that after their recapture it had made it that much harder to view them in their cages; perhaps that was the cruelty of it. She hated now to watch their frantic flapping sometimes violent against the bars. She had heard of captive birds whose wings were clipped but . . . *How could they?*

On this propitious wedding day, upon mounting the French *chifonnier* (forbidden), the girl's quick eye flitting caught sight of the Celestial boy again. This time there was an oily old Chinamen with him who held the young coolie stranglingly up by the back of the collar.

It was striking that the old man still wore the queue snake-like down his back, the square-ish blue cap that was seldom seen now in Paradise. She glanced down just in time to see the boy's slender young hand being shoved shoved down at the elbow by the queerly queued man down through the narrow top opening of a rusty old can and then—to her abject horror—pulled violently up again stripping the boy's forearm of flesh, ripped in a jagged line through the wrist. This solved the mystery of why she had seen the odd China boy wearing a can on his hand before, but Leonora no longer found it amusing.

Leonor-a Nori 'tori neri! Come right now to me! *Goier-a. Jun bear.* Go up to her. Go now!

Obstinate, preternaturally stubborn, the little girl had learned to filter out the voices down below if she could. She drowned them out this time given that the chiffonier, what they called "high boy" (which she thought so funny now) was her goal. Easily, if she worked very quietly with the drawers as step ladder she could climb; ascend, she knew she could.

Arin ariñe, quick, Go get her, son!

The voices would fade if she willed it, would cease three stories below if she wished to banish them from her thoughts, from her will. *Zast!* just like that: it was easy when she put her mind to it. The downtown hotel, in all its four-storied glory was her private castle, but castles must be fortresses too: built to keep out the rif and the raf, her Uncle Noodle at the Ritz once said. (Uncle Noodle was wise. He just spoke English funny like he had oatmeal and marbles rolling round the words.) She, Leonora, was Jin Princess of Echevarria, mistress of the house: all enchantment sprung from *her*.

Leo-Norá*! Noriiii!*

Jendillak, the big people, could be so peculiar. The only time they really made sense was a few days after someone had died and at funerals, only then that the big people were ever alive. That's why the festival of all lamentations and regret called "Death" was good for everyone. After too much meat and wine and coffee, each living soul would leave Echevarria's weary with living (*mais contents*) going home after the funeral feast. After all, it was not they who had departed.

The littlest princess sits in the center of all bird song, now looks down on the street before the song ceases. Tooleriríí tout tout *Tsssst* . . . ! as the Chinaboy looks up unto her. (For some time now this had been her plan.) *Mendietara* to reach as far as high mountains. *Errubietarraiñoo!* As far as the Rubies. She dreams now of their pack-horsed, tented love: of Aita and Leonora only. Every evening, every dawn here caged in Echevarria's, kept with the birds in the sunroom penthouse, Leonora longs for the sky: to be the lover of mountains, to fly right off her mother's precious balcony, across the alley, beyond the flat top roof of Chin's Café where her odd boy lives. Leonora dreams to be with Basajaun wild with Mari in her cave again. To be freeeeeeee pppur-rrr-r-r ooee howwwweee! *I I I will call you "Elora,"* in the alley he'd said. Aie Aie Aie Ama.

Before jumping, she had planned to loose the birds again—her beloveds—for a split second only she thinks of the risk of paradise lost: the deep bosom comfort of her mother's breast, ladies fingers from the French Bakery, the lace of fine dresses, Aita telling stories by a campfire. *Izarrrrák!* The stars cut like wounds in her head, the snow-capped Rubies there before her beckoning. Her Chinaboy Lee, down in the alley who at that very moment was dreaming of her—Leonora—

conjuring her unto him. As the boy stood looking up to the heavens hoping to catch a glimpse of her shape in the high solarium, the girl fell birdlike so fast he knew not what had hit him. *Down the blue mountain in the evening/Between us we forgot the world . . . We walked the long road of the River of Stars.*

At the moment of impact, the coolie boy lifts his arms up up up to the lazuline sky as hers, Leonora's, like the wings of a white dove breaking, bend like two commas as she falls unto him. Miraculously in one swooped motion, Lee catches the butterfly girl as her body plummets down down down flapping mad gorgeous, her petal-like skirt inverted like a water lily afloat on the sky. As she falls into his arms breaking them both quite perfectly, Leonora herself is thinking only of flight. Of how by this evening she will have reached her heart's desire despite their dire warnings. And she would live to tell it in her own very I-told-you-so-I-do-too-know-everything delicious style. At this moment she was preparing to tell all.

It was then her body became him, smashing his thorax and bursting his spleen, she, Leonora, knew she had saved him for herself. The boy, Lee, knew nothing now but the still liminal trench of the near dying.

Bloodied, the child's hand like a claw gripped their fate in the ribbon-like chords of his neck leading to their hearts. Out on the street in a back alley of Paradise *her boat turns back without waiting moonrise/to the royal house amid amorous sighs.* The girl holds on for dear life—for mercy, as the boy pledges her troth, his fidelity. Then with a twist of her wrist so tightly, so surely she finishes him as he wishes to be finished.

Felix culpa. Fait accompli. It is done. Elora and her Lee.

Tybo Weekly Sun, November 24, 1877

Laws have been enacted for the suppression of this traffic, yet we seldom hear of an arrest being made. It may be that our officers are not aware that whites frequent these dens, yet the fact stares us in the face and cannot be denied. Earnest and decisive steps should be taken toward the suppression of the vice and the punishment of the heathen who are engaged in the fearful traffic. Let severe measures be adopted and the sale of the drug will soon be suppressed.

Echeverria's

Here we are. *Hemen gire.* Room 1-2-3. It's that simple. *You may come to tea with me Elias Elí, when you are off your crazy medicine that makes you sleep too much. Berriz? Again? I never knew a boy to pee so well. Here's a bottle. I'll put it in the alley again. Maybe that ugly Chin will drink it for his afternoon tea!* proclaimed the little princess.

By 1922 the prospects of the *etxeko jauna*, Pedro Echevarria, had paid off: even the mining claims were turning up pay dirt. Admittedly, some business deals had gone decidedly south with the changes after the Great War and there was still Prohibition—the greatest of threats to a restauranteur and barkeep, but overall, Peto had hedged bets enough for his major stakes in Paradise to prove profitable. In the end nothing in life is ever perfect, not even in Paradise.

It was she she she! Something like the deadbolt on the stockroom door had shut him out from her. *Auxe bizije!* Such was life, full of conundrum and indignities. It was his wife who never let Peto forget that it was *her* uncle's money that was the foundation of *his* house. The source of Echevarria's was *her* family. Now when things had been going relatively well between them it was *she*, Goya, who insisted on taking the half-witted Chinese boy in.

> *Ze ba*? Why did you move supplies from the storage room?
> For . . . Lee.
> *Zertarako, hembra*? What for, woman?
> To keep him. It's his room now, for a while.
> This Chinaboy?
> *Etxekoa*. He is of this house, Echevarria.
> *Zelako bullshitau*?
> He saved her life.
> *Ezetz*. No. You will not do this.
> It is downstairs closest the bathroom.
> *Or konpon*. Leave it, female woman.
> I have paid for him.
> Paid for him?
> It was the only way.

Thinking, thinking. He would figure this one out. For now, he would leave the bar to Castor, take a nice evening walk along the river by the tracks. He would not return for hours. Perhaps tonight not at all! *Alaxe* just like that he would show her. Make her think twice about this madness of the broken Chinee boy they called Lee. It most probably wasn't even his name, this half-bred dirty tramp. They were *all* Lee in the end now, weren't they?

They say it is an ill wind that blows nobody no good and Gregoria Malasechevarria Echevarria recognized an opportunity when she saw one. She knew that for the boy to stay her husband would require all sorts of extra feminine ministrations: her baking increased, she took more pains with her coiffure and her wardrobe. She even lost some weight, which provided her now with something of a waist. Peto, in this provisional glory as firstborn child, now took happy refuge snuggled within his wife's quite ample bosom and newly restored connubial affections. In this halcyon time, they were happy. Even he began to appreciate the unforeseen advantages of harboring a busted up Chinese wretch at Hotel Echevarria.

Initially, Lee could not move on his own. Dr. Sammy Feinhandler (who was the only doctor in Paradise who would touch Chinese or Indians) had insisted on complete traction and minimal movement. Lee knew he must surrender to them if he wanted to live. *Did he?* Six weeks, then another two perhaps before he could hope for good use of at least his left arm, then maybe use his right: an eternity! This unmoving for him was far worse than the constant activity with the many masters: first in the mines, then with Wing Lee, with Chin, with the old cook at the Spanish Ranch. Not even the knife fight had been this bad. He was as set back by care and attention as much as by the total lack of it! Unlike cruelty, he would come to discover that the silken strong tethers of love were glossy but tight cutting—nearly inescapable.

Before the accident Lee had had one friend whose name was John Joe Johnny, an older boy almost a man, whose fate was nearly as compromised as Lee's. John Joe Johnny's job (who was never called by any shorter name) was now taking care of the chamber pot business at Echevarria's: at first a decidedly compromised endeavor. The broad-backed Shoshone undertook his work with the kindness of someone who himself has known more than once what it means to become incapacitated. The Indian was ever vigilant, but largely silent, which suited Lee. John Joe Johnny himself thought that he had died and gone to heaven living at

Echevarria's: three squares a day (glorious white bread in a bowl of sweetened coffee milk every morning!), a warm bed—and wonder of wonders—a player piano! Temporarily relieved of his duties during the afternoons when Lee had slipped off into a nap, the proverbially creeping Indian would slink into the reception room *serbidora* and quietly cozy up to the self-playing pianola like a dog in winter to a warm coal stove. At least once a week, John Joe Johnny and the bartender Castor would carry Lee, who could not walk, out to the dining room in a sling contraption made of ropes and canvas—his overly tall, but yet emaciated frame balanced between them so that he could accustom himself to polite, human company.

For their part, Echevarria and company had done everything possible for their perfect Chinese oddity. Gregoria had brought in a metal boarders' bed from upstairs lovingly laying it with fresh linen and warm blankets. (Even though Lee himself had laundered more than his share of linen at Chen's Laundry & Mercantile, he had never had it for himself on his own bed no less.) There was an eiderdown pillow complete with pillowcase whose border had been delicately tatted with fine Belgian lace. (He would ask Elora to find a flour sack cloth in the alternate storeroom to replace it before he dirtied it irremediably.) Like the rich man that he now was, Lee continued to take inventory of the room. Slowly, very slowly, he lingered over the many objects of this fortuitous boon.

But for all their good intentions, the parade of gifts embarrassed him: a new cake of lavender soap, a toothbrush, a tin of powdered tooth wash! Now, his own glass vase and flowers brought by Leonora, useless books that represented a new albeit alien world. *Silly Lee. You can't read!* There were curtains on the window and iron hooks painted white for his clothes, and to his utmost shame there was a wide round rimmed basin of a chamber pot. What was wrong with outside? With the alley? Running water was in the adjacent bathroom, a tap and another commode; a "thunder mug" (which is what they called the barbarous thing) ready next door. Stretching up in the narrow bed he could see outside into the alley and down the street to the depot. With the window opened he set his daytime eyes upon a small courtyard of sunlight, red geraniums, a mop. Fresh air and light now permeated his days. He had been bought into the house of Echevarria as one of their own, but at times his good fortune was simply too much for the simple servant boy who had always served others and never learned how to be served.

Mornings, Leonora would come to relate to him a serialized flapper girl tale Aita had read to her from *The Free Press.* Or she would tell him a whim of hers, a joke she had quite proudly collected on the outside: her little gifts, her tender mercies—his school girl Scheherazade. Some days Mintxo would come read to him the newspaper; Grace and Amelia had started *Call of the Wild*, which he loved with a passion. The first thing he'd do as a free man would be to get himself a dog.

Until then, all his other needs were adequately attended to, even his incipient education: they brought him a dictionary and a *McGuffy's Reader*, an arithmetic primer, even an old high school botany text with diagrams and illustrations as month two turned unaccountably into month three.

Silly Lee. You can't read!

You no too, Elora.

Why not?

Because you are five?

I am six! Because you're . . . you're a Chi-nese hea-then with your stupid picture letters and your squinty eyes!

I learn American writing first. Ama say I quick!

She is not your Ama! You are Chinese—a foreign thing.

You parents, born American, Leonora?

Of course we're American. We are Basque and we all go to school! You will never go to school, Elias E-Lee. There are no Chinese there, no coolie boys like you.

After a month or two, Goya thought Lee was coming around and the lady of the house began to administer less and less opium tincture allowing him sips of sweet wine. There was certainly nothing wrong with the boy's appetite! *He eats like an army*, Goya quite happily proclaimed. It was a good, albeit provisional existence: Everyone knew it could not last. Sometimes, at sunset the lift of daytime distractions would fade, and Lee would settle into a sweet half-delirious anticipation of her visit, signaled simply by a different noise in the kitchen, her fast footfall in the hall. Sometimes Lee would lie there waiting for hours, writhing in pain.

Occasionally, the Chinese patient would entertain himself watching the tiny, stinging piss ants engaged in their Lilliputian battles on the window ledge. He watched them slither and pull, marching to the sea set loose upon themselves in the filed lines of their own regimentations. Just when he thought he had deduced their strategies poof! they'd disappear slip away out of sunlight into yet another downward crack. Or was "they," still *they*? They all looked the same. Or did "they"?

Despite their mutual bickering, it was Leonora herself who spent most of the time with her Elias E-Lee. *What was better than your very own China boy?* She had painstakingly fashioned him a window box greenhouse. Naming it their "Chinese Garden" she had quite garishly painted it green with white orbs then placed it on the window sash with *ikuriñak*, tiny Basque-looking flags made of napkins and red bar swizzles. The big box that looked like a mini coffin was soon full of peppers, tomatoes and yellow pokey daffodils too tall! Despite the great pain between tinctures, Lee was content with their Lilliputian kingdom. He liked being the undisputed giant king of a vastly shrunken universe. He was here. He had her—for now, Paradise. But at night it was the black box dreaming, the nightmared hangover from the drug and alcohol that had at first been difficult to monitor with three or four caretakers daily that had almost become his undoing. During the day he lay awake or napping and the time like a river washed over him. But at night, he was locked in the black box of his own remembering, snapped shut in the interlocking Chinese hell boxes of his childhood. For present heartburn there was Pepto-Bismo. For past heartache, no remedy. Only the going through it.

But as time went on, as it has a habit of doing, Lee's mind grew unbearably restless. *Gau mehng á!* What was he to do? He could not move. He could not read under the influences of the wine and the laudanum. He could not write. The doctor and Goya had fashioned an odd sort of traction for both his arms that suspended them parallel out like wings from his too lean torso and made him look like some cock-eyed guardian angel. He must be quite a sight *bai gau fo!* Shit! How was he to endure this soft new hell?

Take heart, E-Lee. Eingo zu, said Gregoria Aboitiz Malasechevarria. You shall live until you die. *Bizi hil arte, mutiko,* my son.
Yong yuan, Ama. Mother, I live for you.
Yong heng for always forever.
Little did they know that it would be old Widow Mallory who would finally save him from himself: Poor Mary Frances Mallory who had no children, no Paradise kin—who had lost her small shack and now desperately needed a way to make something of a living. Around Thanksgiving, Goya invited the elderly spinster (nonetheless ever "Widow" to the Paradiseans) to live in at Echevarrria's: odd jobs and caring for Lee in exchange for room and board. In due time, Lee became her deliverance and her hope—her stillborn son. Every Monday she ran back and forth, forth and back down the street to avail herself of the generous subscription to the Paradise County Library which Goya (privately ashamed of her own illiteracy but not brave enough to address it) had opened in the Anglo woman's name. *Too much reading mixes the brains of women,* her now well-read husband had informed her when she asked him about improving her English: His teaching *her* to read in the mornings turned out to be unthinkable. But for Lee, the long stretches of empty time proved to be fortuitous. Under Miss Mallory's constant ministrations within a year's time with nothing else to occupy him, Lee learned to read very very well. This, it turned out, caused yet another problem.

Everyone in Paradise knew the rags-to-riches miracle fable of Pedro Echevarria: a poor, illiterate peasant boy who came indentured with only the shirt on his back who against all odds had taught himself to read and came to own half the town of Paradise! Up all those years at four a.m. before the rest of the household to light the stove and sit with yesterday's newspaper (or last week's or even the paper of the month before). There, in the dark hours before dawn painstakingly bent on deciphering the strange configurations of letters until they made words, and then the words sentences and the sentences a story. Undoubtedly, it had taken him additional years to crack the code of English and master it all alone. A proud man, Pedro was anything if not determined and preferred his shortcomings to remain very private. Lee's progress did more than astound him; it challenged his position as hero.

What Peto had accomplished in years and years straining over *The Free Press* and *The Reno Evening Gazette*, Lee had mastered in months. (And Peto'd thought them all no better than chimps.) It was curious strange indeed that in time both Pedro and Leonora would become the victims of the green-eyed monster of jealousy: Leonora, of old Widow Mallory and Peto of Lee. With no need for Miss Mallory there would be no need for Lee. Unbeknownst to one other and at tragic cross purposes, each conspired to get rid of their own individual nemesis at great personal loss: Pedro would lose his French-laundered shirts with his wife's sweet affections, and Leonora would lose her in-house Lee.

Tu nah mug a hoy.

Whatever that means, *inpernua jun*! Go straight to hell Chinaboy Lee! The sound of what you say is quite horrible.

Hai m'haih.

You've gone and said it now! Hateful hateful alley cat boy! You will never read to me.

One-day Lee read. To-day, he tell Elora story.

(*Hóu.* I am here because I have come, Princess. *Hemen gire etorri garalako.* Why must I love you you you?)

The Princess of the Tung Lake

Long ago in ancient China, a general was fishing on the Tung Lake. When he spied a huge fish swimming beneath the surface of the lake, he shot an arrow and wounded the creature in the back.

The fish was pulled out of the water and attached to the mast of the ship. But the general's servant, a young man named Chen Pichiao, could not bear to watch the fish dangle helplessly in the air.

"There is something about this fish that fills my heart with sympathy," he said to the general. "May I please put it back in the water?"

Chen persisted until finally the general agreed to let the fish go. Chen was so concerned about the fish he even put a plaster on its wound before lowering it back into the Tung Lake.

A year later, Chen was crossing the Tung Lake alone, and his small boat was caught in a sudden squall. As the boat began to sink, Chen saved himself by clinging to a bamboo crate. After drifting all night, he heard the galloping of horses.

Chen quickly hid behind a tree just as a beautiful princess rode by. She wore a crown of pheasant's feathers and carried a bow and arrow. Behind her rode a host of lovely attendants, also carrying bows and arrows.

As the hunting party galloped on, Chen trembled with amazement. What strange land was this? he wondered.

Chen hurried away from the shore. He traveled over the green hills until he came upon a palace surrounded by high walls. He crossed a stone bridge and ran up a winding path to a red door. Then he opened the door and stepped into a courtyard.

The air was filled with the fragrance of flowers. Bird song came from the swaying willows and tall elms. A swing seemed to be hanging from the clouds.

As Chen wandered the grounds, he heard galloping. The hunting party had returned! He hid behind a bush and watched the princess led her attendants into the courtyard. Her hair was like a cloud of dark mist. As her entourage served fragrant tea, they glittered about her like beautiful embroidery.

After tea, the princess climbed into the swing. Chen nearly fainted with admiration as he watched her swing high into the fleecy clouds, as light as a swallow. After a while, the princess stopped swinging, and she and her attendants wandered away.

In a daze, Chen tried to follow them. But suddenly he heard guards, and before he could hide, the guards captured him and imprisoned him in a locked room.

Chen waited alone in his prison, certain he would be put to death. He imagined that anyone caught spying upon the princess would be greatly punished.

After a day and night of fearful waiting, Chen was escorted to the Great Hall. The guards drew aside a bamboo curtain and announced him to the princess. Chen trembled with fear, for he expected that in the next moment the enchanting princess would sentence him to die.

But the moment the princess laid eyes on Chen, she could only stare in utter astonishment. "Please excuse the rudeness of my guards," she said softly. "And please accept my love and gratitude."

Chen could not believe his ears. "But why, magnificent one, do you spare me?" he asked.

"Last year as I was traveling over the surface of the water," the princess explained, "I was suddenly wounded by an arrow. But you saved me. You even put a plaster on my wound. For this reason, I am indebted to you forever," she said.

"Oh, how wonderful," he said.

The princess then ordered her servants to pour wine

and serve a great feast. The whole place was lit with colored lamps. Bands played; and beautiful mats were laid down for dancing.

As Chen danced with the lake princess, he said, "You need never worry again about your debt to me. Having you as my friend is the greatest reward of all."

Chen Pichiao cared deeply for the lake princess. But after three days, he began to worry about his life back home. In fact, he was certain all his family and friends would be grieving over his absence.

"I want you to live with your human family," said the lake princess, "but I will make it possible for you to visit with me also."

The next day it surprised everyone in Chen's village to see him ride up on a splendid horse. He wore handsome clothes and carried many valuable jewels. From that time on, Chen kept a magnificent home. He often told his relatives and his friends about his adventures with the princess of the Tung Lake. Though everyone enjoyed his stories, no one really believed them.

But then one day a man from Chen's village named Liang was crossing the Tung Lake. Suddenly Liang saw an ornamental barge with carved woodwork and red windows. He heard music and singing. When he peeked into the barge he saw none other than his friend Chen sitting with the lake princess.

"Chen! It is you!" said Liang.

"Why are you so surprised, friend?" said Chen. "I have been telling everyone all along about my life on the Tung Lake."

"But, but," sputtered Liang.

"Won't you join us for wine and food?" said the princess.

Liang visited several hours with Chen and the lake princess. "I must be on my way, now," he said.

"Please say hello to my wife and family," said Chen.
"Indeed," said Liang, a bit dazed. "This news will surprise them all, I'm sure."
Liang said good-bye and headed for home.
But as soon as Liang stepped foot in his own village, whom should he see but Chen! Drinking with a party of friends in the local tea house!
"How did you get back home before me?" cried Liang.
"I don't know what you mean," said Chen. "I have been here all day."
"No you haven't!" said Liang. "I saw you on the lake with the princess!"
"You are mistaken. Chen has been here all day with us," said one of Chen's friends.
"Indeed he has," said another.
"No! No! He can't be in two places at once!" Liang shouted.
As Liang kept ranting and raving, everyone only laughed and told him he was crazy.
After many years of a long and happy life, Chen passed away at the age of eighty. When his coffin bearers carried his coffin to its grave, they thought it was remarkably light. They opened it, and found his body had disappeared. In its place was a bit of seaweed and some water. The coffin bearers gasped in astonishment. "The lake princess must have worked her final magic," whispered Liang.

The final solution (and salvation) of the Echevarria marriage came around Chinese New Year's. Old Wung Lu of the French Chinese Laundry finally died, and it appeared for a time that there would be no one to take over the prosperous business. Lee had already begun his life's mission to become the "fixer" of Echevarria's: his first enterprise to do all its laundry. Ironically,

Wung Lu's death had not only given Lee purpose, it would fulfill the three parts of his life's mission determined during the long months of convalescence. The knight's first quest was to gain proper use of his arms, hands, and legs. The second was to scale the mountains of Echevarria laundry for Gregoria. The third would be the culmination of the first two: pledged to this house, this name, Echevarria, this once and only kingdom, he would fight for Leonora to his death. Bring her great riches from foreign sallies and conquests. When offered it, Elias Elí, also known as Lee, would take his Chinaman's chance.

Ze ba, gixon? What the hell, man?

I bought the laundry for him. Put it in his "uncle's" name under me. They're my silent partners. Pledged to do all the work, reap some of the profits, and shut the fuck up.

Bai-uh! You bought it for *him?* she countered incredulous.

It was the only way.

Zertarako? Whatever for?

We'll be doing more than laundry. It will prove profitable. What we now need is profit. And he's out of my house!

Zure etxea? Your house?

> *In Chinaland there was a man*
> *His name was Chicker Acker Cho Chay Chan*
> *His toes were short and his feet were long*
> *And this is the way the poor Chinaman would*
> *talk. . .*

Chi Keli de le delo in a china wa chikeli de li delo,
In a chinawa china ki in a banana go wachi ow
ow ow!

1932

They used to tell me I was building a dream.
Once I built a tower up to the sun
Brick and rivet and lime.

Prohibak datoz! *Federal agents. Hurry, Run to the cellar!*
We'll be down shoveling coal.

Echevarria's is a flurry of frantic activity—the
whiskey bottle snatched fast from the the pocket of
the overcoat hanging on a hook in the downstairs
bathroom, two gallons of wine hidden in stone crocks
down the drain, three bottles of *pacharán* wrapped in
linens in Gregoria's hope chest now gone. Yet another
bottle of moonshine (God knows what its provenance)
snatched from the false wall in the high solarium. Finally, the cases of beer (not so "near") secured in the
stockroom concealed by boxes upon boxes of pastas
and pastas, cans of tomatoes, and sacks of beans: Everything finally hidden, stacked and properly in place
in the big, four-story bricked hotel.

Luckily, at the first sign of trouble Gregoria had
phoned The Ritz Bar on the party line: *No chickens on*

Sunday. We got company. The last time they'd been raid-
ed—a year past now—Pedro had gone to jail for over a
month. It had taken all his varied poker game connections (which were considerable): Judge Tabor, Doc Gallagher, even Charlie Sewell, to get a reduced sentence
and spring him on his own recognizance as an otherwise upstanding citizen and prominent businessman
of Paradise. *Zer ein ba?* What to do? There was no hotel
business without wine, no breaking even without a bar
however covert.

Down in the cellar Leonora and Elizabeth rum-
maged hurriedly among the provisions making certain there were no "live spirits" other than ghosts. As
children they had spent many an hour in *el subterráneo*
with their father protector who knew all, Elias E-Lee.
The roaring furnace was their dragon. The bedrolls of
the sheepers and a saddle or two their garrison; the
bottles and jars of preserves, the colorful medicinal
tonics put up by Goya, the stained glass windows of
the castle of their own imagining. Much to Elizabeth's
chagrin, Leonora was always the princess: Lee her sav-
ior. She, poor plain Lizzie, the other bit parts according
to their whim. No matter. She was youngest without a
real family. To Echevarria's she had been admitted.

It had all happened to everyone in Paradise many
times before—this business with the Prohibes. Even
to Uncle Noodle and Oly who were Americans and
"tough customers" as Aita said. It was the entire town
of Paradise who got drunk. Grown-ups who made stupid laws and went to jail. (All of this inconceivable to
them.) Everyone drank alcohol in Paradise except for
the Baptist ladies, Presbyterian ladies they imagined,
maybe Annie Foreman's father who was dyspeptic any
ways. There were three Mormon families who kept to

themselves farming, and some old Indians who everyone else said shouldn't drink anyway. This Prohibition thing didn't make good sense to the three of them, but not much the *jentillak* giant folk ever did. *Ixilik egon!* Stay still. *Quiet down there below!* the baritone voice rumbled from upstairs. (Both of them knew who *that* was).

As the girls moved some of the bigger crates full of the belongings of sheepers—back in Europe still out on the range or permanently underground, Leonora spotted something under the largest crate that hadn't been moved in quite some time. The bones of a cat? Or was it something living. Something real?

Look, there Lizzie!

Oh. My. God. The red-headed girl said panting on the dirt like some pregnant cat whose time had almost come.

It's not Muffy Beltza, is it Liz?

It's not a cat at all, Nora.

Let's wait until Lee gets back. I'm not touching it!

Ignoring her friend, Elizabeth fingered the frizzy ends of one too tight pigtail while she compulsively dug at the hard panned dirt with the tip of her pointed shoe.

It's a . . . it's a human baby! *Or it would have been.*

Wait for Lee. Wait for Lee! the older girl caterwauled. He'll know what to do what to do to do, she repeated stupidly. What are you doing, Lizard? all but shouted Leonora.

I'm digging her up. We have to bury her decent. Don't you know anything, Nora?

Think. Think. We must think now, Leonora ordered. Do you want them finding this? Well, do you?

How 'bout we stash it in the bottom of the potato bin?

Don't be ridiculous. Give me that bushel basket now!

Closely observing her fresh-faced sister, Nora took a moment to breathe in, then out, then in again all the while thinking. Although she sensed they shouldn't be doing anything without Lee who was oldest, she handed Elizabeth the big basket, then looked aghast at the younger girl as Liz lovingly extricated the tiny, delicate skeleton from the earthen floor beneath the huge crate like some midwife paleontologist.

There now. See? She's beautiful! Elizabeth exclaimed.

It's dead, Elizzie! How do you know she's a she? the elder sister protested.

Women's secrets. We just know these things, Nora. We have to bury her decent now. Then we are bound to this secret forever. Do you understand? the younger girl asked taking on for once a major role in the play.

Who, whose is she then, Elizzie?

Our baby now between us, our secret and Lee's.

By the time the overly earnest young man had made his way down the steep cellar stairs taking the steps two-by-two, the girls were already balancing an innocuous looking basket between them holding the leather side handles. It appeared to contain something very heavy, something clinking like glass bottles or jars. Lee himself was somewhat baffled by the picture given the fact that for the past few hours everyone in downtown Paradise had been frantically engaged in hiding glass bottles or jars, not readying them to be paraded about upstairs.

What are you two doing? Lee admonished them bemused, suspecting some lightly foul play.

Why, taking peaches up to the kitchen. What else in the world does it look like? answered Leonora, Queen of the May.

Peaches? Those peaches are preserved in alcohol, Elora. *Pas du tout.* I'm afraid they are no good now. A regular public health hazard if you ask me. Lucky for us all that Lizzie and I discovered them. Bad, just gone bad—cloudy and ominous. We're taking them up to the kitchen to assure that no one eats them by mistake, Lee. Donchya know?

He knew alright. He knew her like the lines of the fissured scar on the back of his right hand. Even though Leonora had pronounced the finality of that ever phrase at the end—her typically imperious "Donchya know?" He also knew from Elizabeth's disingenuous face that something was up. Too tall now to crouch down in the tunnel behind the flour and sugar cabinet that led across the alley to Chin's Café, their only line of defense now as young adult citizens of Paradise (even though Elise was still just twelve) was to walk up the stairs, out in the open into the kitchen and out the *serbidora* which was now the only place to hide.

Are you sure, Leonora? he asked directly looking into the luminous face now with sweat beading.

I've never been so sure of anything in my life, Lee. These peaches are going to the dump. We're turning them underground then notifying the proper public health sanatorium. (How she hated it when he called her fully by her name. She was Elora Ora to his Elias Elí!)

That's sanitarian, Elora, he gently corrected her. I think you've got the order reversed. We should notify the proper authorities first, he continued gaining courage, momentum.

Lizzie and I will take care of it, she countered most definitively with her black queen.

No big deal. Right, Elizabeth? he asked the other girl.

For once, listen to her, Lee. Hey we'll dig a hole to China or you can mail the remains to China like you did that Joy Goy guy, Elizabeth finished her curious proposal as Leonora just glared. (How she hated it when he called her fully by her name.)

What are you talking about, Elise? That's not even funny! the young man sputtered, by now quite put out by the two of them.

Come on. *Goizen, mutiko.* Less go, boy. Leonora again tried to mollify him with the old pet name.

Carefully considering the haughty brunette and the humbler redhead still holding the heavy basket between them, Lee wondered how he could ever deny them anything? They were *etxekoak*, his sisters—family. The three of them together would take the load of peaches up past the Chinese bone yard where the wild dogs dig, take their basket of good fruit gone bad in its juices up to the dumps of Paradise.

Elora
Elias
Elise

I am Ramon

ACT I: SCENE I

(The Ritz Bar: Paradise, Nevada, 1932. Across
the alley from Hotel Echevarria, next to Chin's
Café. A cold day in hell on a blue moon. Marie,
dawn is breaking)

> *I remember, I remember*
> *the state where I was born,*
> *that used to be so wringing wet,*
> *and now is so forlorn.*

Digger Brown's caught the bus, Oly.

To Reno?

Farther, way farther west—

Beth honey, why donchya go over to the hotel
and ask Mrs. Echevarria for some Basco soup.
Here, take her this bottle for her rheumatiz.
Stay there with Leonora awhile, and with Lee.

I wanna play poker, Oncle Oly. Is Noggin comin?

Sure toots. He'll be here when you get back, I
promise. Maybe we'll play Pedro just the three
of us. How'll that be?

Poker and I play the house.

You always wanna play poker and you're starting to beat us. Awright, awright already. Afterwards you gotta wash behind your ears and
brush your teats—your teeth for a damn week
without my naggin. We got a deal?

You always nag any ways. Can I have ice cream after dinner then? Echevarria's has cream from a cow and canned peaches! And Uncle Noggin is telling me the sheepherder story at bedtime, the gamine girl informed her Dutch uncle (who was really somewhat Swedish) all happy girl giggling.

Fine then. Ice cream it is, but don't be a heathen. Thank Mrs. Echevarria and watch your table manners all that napkin stuff, hand in your lap like Oncle Noggin showed ya.

But they eat with bread in their hands. No napkin stuff.

When in Rome.

Huh?

Never you mind Whoopee Ti Yi Yo/Git along little doggie.

Dough-gies, Oncle Oly, baby no-mother calves . . . Janey Hickman says you're going to have to give me up, the girl questioned with a statement.

Give you up? Who is this cheap little tart? the Dutch uncle stated with a question.

Janey Hickman. You know, her father's a policeman. The one tha—

Right-o. And what was Uncle Oly when he was a young buck?

A prize fighter. Weren't you worldwide champeen?

Well, of Crow Wing County anyways.

Is it big?

Is what big, toots?

Crowing County.

Bigger than any Janey Hickman from Paradise, Nevada and her Pussy Papa can even imagine. And your Uncle Oly is bigger than Hicko Hickman and Janey-o.

What's a Pussy, Papa?

A jerk, thas what's it to ya! Hey, knock knock.

Who's there?

Terrify.

Terrify who?

Terrify tissue? And with that the Champion of Crowing County kissed his little girl and tickled her all over.

Oh Oncle Cupcake, you're so silly, so very slob-
berlily, she said holding on to the old sailor's
neck for dear life snuffling like a rabbit into the
secure male den of him.

Out with yas then, and with that the girl skipped
across the alley to eat *baraka salda*, garlic soup
with peach ice cream.

ACT 1: SCENE 2

> *From Pioche to Winnemucca,*
> *It was heaven—Just to think*
> *That it now is really an arid sink*
> *And a man can't get a drink!*

Uncle . . . Cupcake? Jeezus, Oly.

She's a kid, Pongo. What the hell do you expect?

She's an awful big kid. Taller n' you.

An you got an awful big mouth. Didn I hear
your mama callin ya? You like the numbers
eighty and six, do ya?

All you got is eighty-six, barkeep. I didn mean
nothin. She's a good kid. Gimme another beer,
wouja now? So, what happened to Digger? He
catch the bus?

You could say that.

Where's the funeral?

Don know the goddamn details. Devil's in em
though. My guess is over to Echevarria's.

At least there'll be bread and wine.

You got that much right.

ACT 2: SCENE 2

Buddy, can you spare a dime?

Bill Brown's bought the farm, Shakespeare.

The Poor Farm, no doubt.

Reached the ole Sweet Promised Land, awright. Gone west 'n seen the elephant he did.

Unfortunate turn of events. Does Elizabeth know?

I sent her over to Echevarria's. Not like she ever saw much of the sonofabitch, anyways. Maybe it won't even matter.

That sonofabitch was her father.

Some father.

Where's the funeral?

What church would have him? I have a feeling he come to a no good end, Shakes. Do we have to tell her?

We should keep in mind what would be best for Elizabeth.

Haven't we done that since Margaret died? She's all we, I mean, we're all she has now, Shakespeare.

What about those relatives back east?

Right-o. What do we do then? Sit on it awhile?

We must notify the proper authorities.

Ya know what happens to kids when they're orphans?

Oliver Twist?

I ain talkin bout no stuff outa books. I'm talkin about our own Bethy who'll end up with some old sonofabitch of a lecher uncle back in Arkansas on a dirt farm working her fingers to the bone day and night for some fat great aunt with piles and chickens.

The bucolic life is said to be beneficial to children.

Aw, get off it, ya queer limey.

I thought you told me to "sit on it."

Admit it, Shakes. You're as scared as I am. You wanna turn Bethy over to the state? This state? You ever been to a state children's home, an orphanage?

Spare me the gruesome details.

Trust me, I know. Bethy's not leavin if my name isn't Olav Armundson. Hey, whazup? You're too quiet. You on the sauce again?

Ah happy-go-lucky me
and broken-hearted you . . .

Turn that goddamn thing off, will ya?

It isn't fair
for you to fill me with dreams
that can't come true . . . uu oo uuoo

This is serious business, Mister.

To taunt me / To want me . . .

All right! D'accord. We keep Elizabeth.

If it's just for today . . .

You agree? Arenchya gonna give me a run for
my money? Quote me a buncha book stuff and
go all . . .

The day I hear you say / You were lucky
too.

. . . purple in the face? Slam down your fist on
the bar 'n shout, I turn deaf ears! Fait accompli!? Hey, whachya lookin at any way?

"A woman's face with nature's own
hand painted,

Hast thou, the master mistress of my
passion."

What the hell? That's not funny. You
listenin to me?

"A man in hue, all hues in his controlling

Much steals men's eyes and women's
souls amazeth."

You don't give a shit, do ya—about Beth, I mean? You never give in until you get a big row out of it. Admit it an stop with the goddamn Shakespeare, Shakespeare!

I admit no such thing. And you, my dear misguided friend, if you had any sense at all, you would refrain from such rash conjecture and come to the realization that after all I . . . I

Jeezus, you're not gonna up an start bawlin again now, are ya? I hate that shit. Get a hold of yourself, man.

Very well then, state law most clearly states—

Fuck state law. We're not gonna give her up, our Beth.

You think a court of law is prepared to give a twelve-year-old girl to a pair of . . . gentlemen like us, do you, Pantagruel?

What kinda relatives you think Digs got on his side?

The Duke of Wales, maybe? Ma Joad? Florence Fuckin Nightingrail. I turn deaf ears.

Tell me what you're sayin in plain English, man. How is it that an Englishman can't speak English?! I'm not foolin now. This is important. For Bethy.

Para Elisa, fur Elise. For the record, Elizabeth Brown Barrett lives at Hotel Echevarria and visits The Ritz sometimes for, tutoring—for

Latin and philosophy. The Echevarrias will be her "real" adoptive parents bonafide by state law since they have the money (even though they *are* Catholic), and we shall be her, uh, "fairy godfathers" purveyors of French, Latin, fast affections, and Geometries! What the girl needs is good grammar, not a good home, *comme on dit. Alors,* lights out, my good man. I turn deaf ears. *Fait accompli!* You do intend to feed the alley cats out back, do you not?

I souped em at noon, but there's still two out there.

Give them quarter.

I thought it was only a dime?

Hard times. Hard Times. This is the worst of times and the worst of times. There is a wisdom of the head and a wisdom of the heart, *mon ami.* When in doubt, the heart, my friend, the heart. And that is all ye need to know.

But since she prick'd thee out for women's pleasure,

Mine be thy love and thy—

Cut the crap already. Is it a plan then? I'll have my sister in Omaha send the postcards so Bethy thinks—

As you will, noble Sancho.

*To find your love is aching / And tears will
fall
As you recall . . .*

You're the queerest limey I ever met, an' thas
sayin' something, Shakespeare.

Comme vous voulez, as you like it, my good good
man. How about a nightcap? Then we go upstairs and flights of angels sing thee to thy sleep.

All my blackberries/Are blueberries now

Act 3 (Curtains)

*Urtxo xuria little white dove,
Why must you leave a heart full of love?*

Elizabeth, it's past nine. Bedtime.

Oncle Oly said we could play poker tonight, Uncle Noggin.

You have your Latin to do yet, Chuck. School
tomorrow.

Why don't you marry Mrs. Echevarria, *mon oncle*?

What's that? Why, she's got a husband—Don
Pedro.

So why don't you marry Connie?

She doesn't want a husband, Precious. She's an
independent.

Will I get a husband, Uncle Noggin?

Most likely.

Do I need one?

We all need someone, Princess. Perhaps just a beau.

How did you find Oncle Oly?

A long and convoluted tale.

Like *The Arabian Nights*?

Précisement. The nightly entertainments of Scheherazade. And thus, Bradamante and Angelica, that time-worn out tale out out damn spot I say tally-ho to the new Orlando's Voyage Out out ohh oh you Hippograff to you Elizabeth, Fur Elise! This Christian Knight Roland Orland errant outlandish Innamorato y Furioso yes yes we must be free!

Are you drunk Unc?

I am just rather tipsy toasty tonight. Warm before the heartache sings. Ah, love itself a kind of insanity. Ariosto got that one right ole *Chanson de Roland* role on role on and on on on and roll on roll one get one on?

I want the sheepherder story, mister.

```
   The Silver State: July 17,1894
An insane Basque sheepherder was ar-
rested yesterday morning and locked
up. He was wandering around town car-
rying a shepherd dog on his back, and
is supposed to have packed the animal
```

all the way from the sheep camp where he was employed, about 40 miles south of here. His insanity seems to be of a religious turn, as since put in jail he spends most of his time muttering prayers, interspersed with howls almost hideous enough to scare a railroad "scab" into being a gentleman.

Not that sad old rag again. So *depriment*.

I want Jean-Baptiste Biscarí!

We all want many things, my dear girl. It is time for bed, lights out, to sleep sleep perchance to dream, fair maiden *ma petite chou à la crème je vais te manger tout cru*.

You will not!

> *Tips his hat just like an English chappie/To a lady with a wealthy pappy/Very strappy—Puttin' on the Ritz.*

Uncle Noggin, do you think I'm too big?

Too big? Too big for what, Sugarplum Fairy?

The boys at school said I was getting 'tits'.

Yes, well, perhaps they're right. Boys are remarkably observant about such things.

How come the other girls don't have big 'tits'?"

Because you're *exceptional, accelerated,* yes, that's it!

Uncle Noggin?

Yes, my dear?

Do you and Oncle Oly love me?

Are the Basques Catholic?" Like my parents I mean?

Like your parents, Beauty. Now shall I tell you a tale or do you wish to continue in your existential quandaries?

I want the sheepherder story.

Don't you have any tales of your own? *Pas de petits amours?* For truth is ever stranger than fiction. Tis true!

Hey, that's my line!

No it isn't. It's Byron. But is it *true?* Truly true?

I'll tell ya what's truly true. *Tu est idiot, mon oncle.*

Mon Dieu! but you're a sassy lass. *Touché! En garde!*

> *Beauty very civilly thanked them that courted her, and told them she was too young to marry, but chose to stay with her father . . .*

Hush, girl. *Tais-toi.* (I like this part).

It's stupid. I want Jean-Baptiste Biscarí.

On second thought, how about *Twice Told Tales?* I'll tell them only once to save time. Hawthorne can be tedious.

They gonna take me away, Uncle Noggin?

Wha—who they going to take away?

I heard the teachers talking. With Digger gone ...

I AM JEAN-BAPTISTE GOYENECHE BISCARI
PLEASE ROUTE ME TO FAUSTINO
BASTARRACHE
ROUTE 1 PARADISE NEVADA AMERICA

What do you mean "gone"?

You know, how he's always on the road. The teachers said The Ritz Bar isn't a fit place for a "child"—that would be me.

Fit for their fat arses, the old bitties. Never fret, Chuck. You realize Uncle Noggin is very very smart and long ago in a land far away he was a ... university professor and a maggot—I mean, magus or magnent. I forget which.

Précisement. Magus from the Persian 'magus', Latin plural 'magus', 'magi' magic magician— not entirely unrelated at that, eh? I, my lass, was a regular Paracelsian in my discipline.

Will that fat lady with the ugly stockings take me then?

Poppycock, falderal and fiddle de dee. Don't worry your pretty little head. And who is always smarter, Reynard the Fox or the chickens?

Why, Renard always out foxes the chickens, but they out-chicken him.

Touché! Indeed, you are your uncle's daughter. That reminds me: two chickens for Mrs. Echevarria this Sunday.

Did you drink whiskey again tonight? You know it makes you crazy.

*Snap your fingers/walk around a bit
shake your shoulders/*

lift your skirt/or lift your pants a bit . . .

Actually, the proper lexeme is "scotch" not "whiskey." Not as in the adjectival "Scotch" whiskey, but as the definitive nominal "scotch," as in "A rose by any other nominalization would smell as sweet," my sweet Juliet-Elise-Elisabet, you bet.

You *are* drunk. I'm gonna tell Oly on ya unless you give me Jean-Baptiste Biscarí.

Drink to me only with thine eyes, Elizabeth Barrett in a Garret Browning *à votre service.*

Puttin' on the Ritz . . .

The herder or I squeal, Buster.

Gaixua Jean-Baptiste Biscari

Battita's head, day-and-night night-and-day, was full of the great white oceans of bleating bleeethering sheeeep bleee bleeee baaaa baaa Baaaaaasque, as the old joke went. Twenty to fifty sheep to a bunch; two to four bunches to a flock; a thousand or two thousand to a band; one to two bands to one man— to one dog if the man were lucky. In a single year a herder would walk a thousand miles or more in a single pair of boots. This precariously accidental arithmetic for Jean-Baptiste Biscarí was in the end to prove tragic. Was this New World high desert transhumance his sweet promised

Biba artzainka eta
Hemen egoiten ahal
direnak

land or was it one sweet promised hell? One thing was certain: the flock held its own internal logic. There was no getting around a flock of sheep, only the going with it. Was it he who herded sheep or the sheep that herded him? Jean-Baptiste Biscarí.

> Man is not the lord of beings. Man is the shepherd of Being.

> *Esperantzarik ezbada itzulzeko atzera / If there is no hope of returning home / Amerikako zuhaitzetan izainda zerbai diona / there will be something left on American trees / Artzain berriak hor ikuskio du zaharraren izena / The young herder sees the names of the old ones written on the trees / horrek erranen dizu lehendik hor ibilli den/ and will know there are Basques who have gone before him*

My pretty little Margarita is a fag

Alone, there was the flock. Alone, there were the mountains. Alone, the trees through which the Ancestors spoke. Alone, only the names. In the forest, along the long valleys, out on the desert the shepherd was alone. Jean-Baptiste Biscarí, *gure* "Battita," would take his secret frozen to the grave with him— the little bones of his long fingers frozen along with nine of his toes. (The cage of his ribs would make a nice rack of lamb for coyotes or wolves, he had once thought to himself.) Now perhaps it had come to be. *Basamortu goiko mendian* in the high desert mountains anything was possible. *Auxe Amerika!* This was America!

He first began to notice the ringing in his ears the second foray out-and-back to town after lambing. Down in town the tall, tin-embossed ceilings of Echevarria's *serbidora* echoed like the devil's anvil in his head. As he tried to eat the food set before him— garlic soup, beef tongue, *menestra de setak kaka zuri*, with *kafié*—the cigarette smoke rose above him in clouded thunder like Michaelangelo's paint heavened Sistine Chapel. The swills and sworls all rising up up up to the American star lariat design *Aupa!* The din of their voices was ever in his eeeaars. Burning his skiiin, their hot molten laughter. The nightmare of their faces all wide-mouthed and open stinging his dreams. *Tintantintantintanabulation.* (That echo in that space behind your eyes all night till you cried—Battitatatata Jean-Baptiste Biscarí.)

The herders, the revelers: the fun all around you. *Aupa, aupa mutil! Echeverria'ra* let's go to town, boy!" up on the mountain they shouted out out out to him. Down in town, *serbidoran* of Echevarria's, the back-slapping jests of French and of Spanish; the simul-linguistic blur of four or five Basque dialects with some broken down English thrown in for good measure. *Aie Ama!* Blessed Mother! This Sheepherder's Ball. Let the feast day linger! Let the party begin! *Kaching cha-ching,* the sweet sound of cash American mo-ney.

The long dinner finished (cheese and apples, grapes in summer on a big, white plate), the serving girls would wipe their hands of it finally on their aprons and pull the chairs aside screeeeching against the marvelous smooth tile the Americanos called lin-oh-lee-um. Then nickelode-on on on on, the girls pulling you to the dance floor after whiskey, the girls pulling you in in in. The coffee, the brandy, the smoking cigars signaled the dancing: the time of hot bodies jostling, the time of all sins. The sweating and shouting. The laughter. The singing. *Aupa! Aupa!* Go round with the dancers *gure Battita!* This was the beginning. *Amaiera hasiera* da. This was his end. *Auxe, asken dantza* this was the last dance. His dance card was emptied. The dancing, the singing were doing him in.

As the young couples coupled, and the lonely cut in, the older sheepers held back, preferring the bar with the hotelkeeper who looked locked like a listening prisoner—his tight vest and tucked tie, the armbands, the long white apron just like in Bilbao or Gay Par—ee! *Zelan du izena, orek?* What was his name? That cock-a-the-walk, Mr. Cockle Doodle Do? *Errrt-uh-err-eu-errr praaketan porrot egingo* he'd bust a gut with that tight strut. He'd lose his shirt someday. *Gaixua* poor man! One day, every man will lose his castle. Every dog has its day. *Or konpon.* This one fact no matter, no mystery. *Ni nas Vizcaytarra/Ni nas pobre bat.* Pedro Echevarria— nothing but a poor Vizcaino.

The same as me.

The riiingiiing in his eeeeeaaars could not be stopped by wine or by women. *Erremediorik b'ezta ere,* for him there was no remedy, no Jesus, Maria or José. There was no other way. In him were the voices, voices hissing incessant. In him the voices were not Basque, not

English, not Spanish or French, not even Chinese. The
voiceless voices were in him night and day. The voices
scratched the insides of his eyeballs like hay.

Hear what we say!
Speak your word and break, is what they would
say.

Now you have heard all, and know why I must return to my forest. Return to the voices of the animals.
Return to Basajauna, Mari. Only where there are graves
are there resurrections like me *aaara rra ruuuah!!*
Irrintziirrikatzen I am Jean-Baptiste Biscariiiiiii!

> Elko Free Press, April 25, 1925
>
> A party consisting of Bart McDermott,
> Dan Sabala and Frank Romano re-
> turned yesterday from a trip to Lib-
> erty Lake in the Ruby Mountains. They
> brought back three beautiful rainbow
> trout The largest weighing about five
> pounds.

It was finally the mountains that had him for lunch.

They found the body of Gaixua Jean-Baptiste
Biscarí come spring about Easter in a grove of near
budding aspens still wedged between two trees. Left
there stark naked with his frozen arms extended out
along the branches like some frontier Western Jesus,
he wasn't going anywhere. (It was such a surprise to
the whiskey-guzzling fishermen, that one of the sports-
men, Dan Sabala, the story goes, gave up drinking right
then and there but nobody knows for sure). Ole Biscarí, "Battita", naked as a jaybird, was gruesomely
spread-eagled between the forking branches of two

low-growing aspen trees. Like some medieval incorruptible, his body was so well preserved there was virtually no decomposition except for the face. Aside from a small wolf-eared black sheep dog that approached the search party, there was no other evidence of company and at the time of the inquest, Sheriff Harris made note that the camp was fully intact with no apparent evidence of foul play. Also that the Basque sheepherder, identified as Jean-Baptiste Biscarí may have died of blood poisoning given the "apparently" self-inflicted wounds gouged into his chest. The ciphers (were they ciphers?) on the torso had at some time festered, the tattoo deepening had healed during the cold, dark winter becoming by spring the tough bark of his skin. Perhaps it had been the festering wound and not hyperthermia, the coroner added, which had been the cause of his death. (Truth was, noted the sheriff, it had been some kinda hell getting the body out of that goddamned tree.) All the way down the mountain without breaking him, back to Paradise, Jean-Baptiste Biscarí.

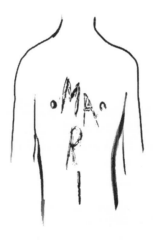

1942

I went to work in an untouched place
I'm sure I meant no blame, sir
But a white man struck me in the face
And told me to leave his claim, sir.
I could not get employ
The Know Nothings would bid me go—
'Twas tu nah mug a hoy.

Ai-ta... Father.
   Pu-ta! Whore! The word single definitive now,
clear.
   Jun hemendik! Get out of here! *Renoko Putaaaaaaa!*
   More coyote crouch than rattlesnake slither, his
voice out on the street was directed like a shotgun directly at her. *Ez—Ech-e-va-rri-a. Ez-etz!* always the
Basque negation. She was Echevarria no more. Leonora turned on her heel away for the last time from
Echevarria's—turned her back on her father's house
that was really her mother's.

The screen door of the hotel bar swung in a hard arc slamming shut. It was hot on the street, very hot. She pulled the bright blue culottes down at the crotch, then removed her glasses wiping them rakishly on the tail of a sailor striped midriff shirt. Leonora lit another Lucky Strike. For a moment only, she looked up at the third window of the second floor of the Nevada Hotel, then pursing her lips around the cigarette—all smoke and Lauren Bacall—Leonora sucked the dry air in.

Goizen! Less go!
Lee's exuberance like a stud colt turned out to pasture unbounded. On this spring day he called out to Leonora all that was theirs meant to be. Fast clutching the metal handles of their red Indian bicycles, they headed out of town on America's shining Victory Highway which connected all points east and west, from sea-to-shining-sea 1932.

Gregoria herself had once justified the purchase of the extravagant cycles to Pedro as "business expenses." (Go talk to your accountant Milton Badt Ass'n) and if he were further inclined to disagree (How could he?) the lord of the manor could go and take his new Packard (pronounced by Goya like Pernod *Ricard* in French) and (in clear American English) "Or you can shovel em up you asses." He could even go fetch the soil-clinging vegetables (*patatak!*) himself at the old spring where the waterworks of Paradise began. Initially, her idea was: *If the boy still can't walk at least he can ride on a red bicycle in this great shiny new America-The-Beautiful.* She would see it it.

Today, the lady-of-the-house had sent them out to Chinese Gardens, panniers strapped about their

bicyles like low slung saddlebags with orders for
the hotel for Old Wang Lung. They were Marco Po-
lo's merchant marauders, camel-back and berobed:
theirs were high adventures. Such pure joy in moving
fast with nowhere to go. Such freedom being young!
And every time—which was often—the old Chinese
gardener-of-Chinese-gardeners would greet them
at the causeway with the same salutation which Lee
translated as something like "You come because I have
been waiting!" Followed always by, "Meezus Goya
fresh frus vegables. House Echevarrí."

For them, Wang Lung would have just picked apple
or a fresh peach in season, always a Confucian saying
at the ready which traditionally began with the phrase
"Good people": *Good people are careful what they say
and moderate in eating and drinking* (just one peach).
Good people accept others with openness (with one peach
or with one apple). *Good people stand without changing
places* (no sitting, there work to do). *Good people pre-
pare weapons to guard against the unexpected* (one eye
on garden one on highway). *Good people comfort others
and urge reciprocity* (your mother Goya my fine friend).
Good people become the same while keeping their difference.

1939. By September the Germans had invaded Poland—
what for them was yet to come? Leonora was twenty-five,
decidedly no maiden. Lee, on the verge of thirty, fully grown and a well-established man in business. But,
with all the trouble in Europe, Leonora and Lee were no
longer young. All of their lives in Paradise seemed provisional, but for them now on furlough from the present in their garden, he holds her to him like a prize. She
was his as they stood east of Paradise and out of time.

By this time, Old Lung had been gone these many years. There was no task master now, for all their fathers were dead to them. The war not yet over. One afternoon in early spring with still a light crust of snow on the ground, Leonora impulsively took the red Indians out of the garage on Court Street without Aita's knowing. Lee had been since banished from Echevarria's for no apparent reason. *Ez ezetz. Ez Echevarria!* someone had shouted, or had it all been a dream? None the wiser, they set out due west in the direction of Chinese Gardens. If not their lives, at the very least their hearts were carefree.

Leonora and Lee were surprised to find the old canals choked dry with undergrowth, with tumbleweeds. What had happened to the red poppies? The lone locust tree that drew the bees? Where the bees? All their *susurrus.*

Lee began to clear the tangle in the ditch with a rusted rake he knew would still be wedged between two spiney Russian olives. He worked on the clearing in the hot sun, sweat etching dust trails down his young back until the heavily leaved dam was loosened, the brambles broken up, and a trickle of clear fresh water once again flowed from the old spring that supplied the town of Paradise. She tended to gathering the brambles and blown trash into a pile: Elora Ora, *Txori-Txoria* little bird. Here, for a final time, the fresh mornings of their childhood were for an afternoon restored. He was twenty-seven and she had turned twenty-two: She was still his Elora. He was still her Elias E-Lee. Their time had come and at once was undone.

The proud desperate young man, his face open as an Asian moon, stood planted there in his stiff imported shoes like a sagebrush denying drought.

Ezkongaikoak. We are promised, by our families, Lee—from our village, from our birth! From the same village in Spain, donchya know? It's tradition. They are Arrascada. We, Echevarria. There is nothing left to do, to him she all but whispered. Nothing but the stone-faced suitor, now no bees their *susurruuusss.*

He looked first into her face, then down at her dusty slim espadrilled feet. As she spoke, he dropped the picnic hamper that had been packed lovingly for them at the Cottage Café by Ramona Dick whose mother had once worked with Lee at the French Chinese Laundry. Lee stood still there before Leonora, facing their final fate. Looked hard down at the ground—a survival action. Being Basque, Leonora refused to do any such thing. Just then, a fat carp surfaced from the spring waters and fast snatched a fly that was airborne still *buzzzing.*

Why won't you marry me, Leonora? he asked her plaintively.

It's illegal, Lee.

(So are we), his silence more telling than any reply.

No other way, Elias E-Lee, her unstinted offering. *There is only Benny and meee,* the echo of her loving lie, carefully fashioned, reverberating.

When darkness descended he no longer held her. She no longer had him. As the lone cars droned on out on blue highways, a northerly mistral chilled them to the bone. In the end, neither of them had been hungry and Lee left the basket for the rabbits, the birds, and finally the coyotes. The cicadas were chirping as bullfrogs croaked out their big bass vibrations from special organs of great verdigris bellies *bellooohwuh.*

There, in the darkness shivering in the gardens of Eden the spirits of dead Chinese gardeners come to pay the young lovers homage and partake of their death offerings. Bent like coolies at the waist on the hardpan desert the coolies are digging, digging halfway to China using their their own thigh bones *Hurry hooome to me / wet with rain / You belong to to me e e.*

345 Court Street

Elko Free Press, October 18, 1941

Announcement was made here today of the sale of the A.W. Hesson home, located at the corner of Seventh and Railroad streets to Mr. and Mrs. Pedro Zubieta. The Zubietas were formerly of Whiterock, where they operated a store. They have sold their interest in the store and will reside in Elko in their newly purchased home.

Before her husband took his leave of her at their uptown house in the best neighborhood in Paradise (Seventh and Court Streets), Gregoria Malasechevarria called out to her Peto from her English gardens. (Or were they, in fact, French and continental?) All anyone in Paradise (which still wasn't a fancy place) knew was that Echevarria's gardens certainly were extravagant (however did she find the time). The pink stone house two-story on Seventh and Court was truly impressive: magisterial and abundant just like its main builder and gardener, Mr. and Mrs.

Nora zoaz, gixontxu? Where to my little man? she called out to her husband this time minding the tone of her manners.

Iñora noe ni. I'm goin nowhere fast, his mortified reply.

(*Internura?* To a funeral?), she wondered. Or to The Palm Saloon: A Gentleman's Bar?

1902

What begins bad, ends bad, *esaten da* the old ones say.

It had all started out as a mistake anyway, that first night with him: the wrong hotel, the wrong man after all. The Central Pacific had been delayed by snow westbound over the Rockies, three hours shut down out of Denver on the cold hard tracks. By 10:02 p.m. Pete Jauregui had given up waiting at the Paradise Depot for the new girl and had gone home. She probably wouldn't be any good for workin anyway. What was the point of a serving girl who wasn't used to serving? he thought to himself throwing down a final smoked cigarette then spitting on the sidewalk to extinguish it. *Inpernua jun da, bai,* the country had gone to hell after the century's turn any way. Even the trains couldn't run on time. He was tired. He was hungry and he had to piss. Tomorrow he'd get someone else who didn't own a hotel to stand out here and wait for a train and a girl that wasn't coming.

Gregoria had not arrived in Paradise on time, but The Palm had closed earlier than usual that snowy April evening in 1902 due to an inventory shortfall and a flood. It was a fateful delay: Pedro Echevarria had time on his hands and money for the houses. Life in Paradise, Nevada was good. At precisely 10:17 it just so happened he found himself standing at the Paradise depot looking up at the platform contemplating going farther west when an unexpected train barreled into the station. *O Fortuna.* The young woman who deboarded the train there right before him had the most arresting eyes, blue eyes like rain. She carried a large leather satchel, behind her the largest steamer trunk he had ever seen (and he'd seen a few). She was quite obviously Basque, yet another immigrant: deeply bosomed with a wide almost beautiful face, something decidedly solid about her. *Hips like these hold many sons,* he told himself watching her descend from the slick metal step off the train. *Bai zera* you betchya. This one certainly fit the bill.

Euzkaldune? Are you Basque? he finally ventured.

Baietz, yes sir, *jauna. Neu naz Bizkaytarrá!* the joyful affirmative, then the more tentative English, I . . . am. (Ha, at the very least she'd called him sir recognizing his lofty Paradise position by his Spanish shoes, all his fine clothes.)

Nobody's fool: Pedro Echevarria kept fingering his hole card deeply sequestered in his trouser pocket. *Onek,* why this one had come not with one but with *two* large steamer trunks all for her own special maintenance! *Gente de algo,* he thought to himself—her people came from something. But then again . . . *What ever was she doing here at the outpost-of-the-outcast-and poor unfortunates?* Even though she was quite evidently Basque, her country was not his poor peasant country. Her provenance certainly not his. Clearly, the language was all that they really shared, at least their dialects were within ten kilometers. *Ala,* would she ask him for help or not? Or could she carry all that *equipaje* herself?

(Pedro was, if nothing else, a very curious man.) The luggage was all so new, so expensive. He knew he'd stick around and see about this high class mystery.

Estar Hotelera? To the Star Hotel? he asked looking at the cloth label hanging by a single thread from her ample bosom.

Bai, jauna. Mecedes. Yes sir, please. (*Aie Ama*, the journey has ended. Why wasn't he attending immediately to her luggage?)

Zu Estar Hoteltarra al zara? Are you of the Star Hotel? she searched his odd gold eyes wondering where they would take her.

No way lady, he said with an overly affected American accent. (She was solid alright, that much was certain—*maciza* fleshed out between the bricks.)

This smallish man before her cut a very fine figure, something in him interested her. Was it intrigue or was it danger? His nose as long as his . . . or was it his dandy American whiskers? *Ura zan gizona ura.*

Hotel Echevarria, finally he proclaimed his provenance and pedigree all too definitively.

Skipping not even the proverbial beat. *Ondo*, fine then she said. *Aurrera!* Take me.

What was the difference? A hotel was a hotel and a man was a man. *Whose woman was she now that Aita had sent her away?* the only remaining question. *What did her name now really matter?* Thinking this, she offered the dapper mustachioed *Amerikanu* the opposing leather handle of one barrel-stave trunk, her feet already pointed down the street in the right direction. Given half a Chinaman's chance, Gregoria Garteizechevarria was a woman who would take two.

Goizen, less go, mister.

1942

Eldu zara, Elias E-Lee, you have come.
Hemen gire etorri garalako, maitea. We are here, my
love, because we have come.

By 1942 all of Europe was under German domina-
tion before Stalingrad—there was nothing left to do.
Now they were all done for. They walked togethered
now down the track north towards the post office.
Turned right, then out in the open past The Palm, by
Paradise Parts, Stinson Berger's Furniture, even by
Anacabe's General Merchandise. On their way to the
courthouse, Leonora and Lee passed Urriola's Standard
Station and Johnny Urriola who'd played the trumpet
to Leonora's sax in high school: a lifetime, so many life-
times ago! The names of the fallen had begun to accu-
mulate around Paradise by early 1942: Vern Archibald,
Peter Etchepare, Adrian Mariluch—no word yet of Pete
Zubieta. One by one, the limbers and caissons rolled on,
as sons and fathers and friends and brothers—their he-
roes rolled into town.

Lee desperately wanted to wipe away the mois-
ture beading on her perfect brow; Leonora longed to
lean into him as she had as a child. Again, they started
walking now down the main street of Paradise. There

was little else a couple could do now in town during the war: JC Penneys, Nevada Bank of Commerce, the Cottage Café—a cup of coffee, a piece of apple pie would be heaven on earth to them to share. Did they dare? To sit with him and look into his eyes, to talk about their pedestrian days or the war as normal people would. To sit there out in the open having pie and maybe coffee, to sit and laugh tell a story would be paradise to Lee and Leonora.

But for now, they grabbed their purloined purchase: a simple stroll about town. He told her he would take her to San Francisco. That he knew *people*: a hotel, breakfast in a coffee shop in the morning with the day's paper in Chinatown. Now walking past Blohm's Jewelry and Gifts, the strikingly handsome couple paused as if on cue in front of the neighboring courthouse at the big weepy Chinese elm which Dave Dotta—still mayor after all these years—had decreed must be removed long before the war. They stopped there together on Main Street at midday their eyes meeting, touching in the open becoming at once all over again. They mourned all the days and years never together, so long ago parted.

It was she who leaned into him first. At last he held her, held on for dear life. With her weight he now remembered catching her like a bird that very first time in the alley, remembered up Fifth Street by the dump in the dark at night as coyotes howled. All he remembered was holding her down *subterraneoan* in the basement, then in Chin's opium dens leaning into the earthen shelves. He had held her at the fairgrounds and at the back of the Gaiety Theater so dangerously once on a Sunday, held her fast in their childhood, thoughout their youth falling ever falling so fast *felix culpa*. He had always held her falling into him.

As for Leonora—heir princess of Echevarria—she had fallen from on high so solidly, so hard fast that first

time unto him there was no extrication, no surgery sepa-
rating the Basque daughter of Echevarria from the heart
of the poor coolie from Chin's Café. A world war was on:
all bets were off now. In the alleyway between the café
and Echevarria's, he held her today again so closely they
both were trembling. With hope now Lee was delirious.
Leonora was his breath, but Lee could not breath.
Leonora, espaldijón! Lon tine no see, eh? Johnny Urriola shouted out to her on the corner of Railroad & Main.
Bai zera. You bet.
They say you were back east, Missouri?
Kansas. Sister of the Sacred Heart, Passion Whatever.
You're an army nurse now then they say.
Navy, *esaten da.* That's what they'd say.
The Basque service station attendant inexplica-
bly ignored Lee, the boy with whom he'd had his first
woman (who at the time was nothing but a girl). They
all knew that Johnny U had been with him that first fast
screw on the steps of the Presbyterian Church on Third
Street. There was no understanding the silence between
the men now but, they all left it at that. No matter. It
was done. They were all said and done. Some of them
were coming home between tours, home at last for a
while. Others coming back in black boxes signed, sealed
and delivered to their door by their good ole Uncle Sam.
Who were they here stateside to question anything?
His hand brushed hers now, the fingers quivering
like the feathers of a bird that had long ago flown. *Bizi
naz ni* because I am living. *Creeek,* as they walked she
listened to the awkward sound of his leather shoes: too
polished, too Italian, too new. How he had dressed for
this day! The neatly laundered cuffs of his expensive
linen shirt, his hair slicked back black shining like an
Arabian sheik. Hers. All their *sussurus*—Elias E-Lee.
I saw Aita this morning, he finally told her.

He talked to you?
At least he didn't take a shot at me this time.
Wheredja see him?
At The Palm, coffee royals as usual. They left the door open because of the heat.
Why didn you go in?
It's a "gentlemen's club," Elora. I'm no gentleman.
That'd make two of us, Lee.

Inauspicious sworls of dust motes circulated in the afternoon sun at the bar of Echevarria's where there was a small five o'clock gathering. For the ladies (who were still ladies) Peto kept *pacharán*—a Basque liqueur made from chokecherries, elder berries, and red currants gleaned from the high canyon trails of the Rubies—beneath the bar. (They could partake of it *serbidoran* in the hotel parlor, thank you very mucho). For the gentlemen, in addition to the ubiquitous what-have-you wine and beer, the supply of good scotch and domestic whiskey was running decidedly low due to additional war rationing (no yeast!) and previous crackdowns on his own diverse production operations (Prohibes). Truth to tell, before this goddamn wet-dry and world war was over, someone some day, was going to drop dead from the bad jack rotgut he (most regrettably) on occasion was forced to serve! Paradise's most prominent *hotelier*-barman-*entrepeneur* dreamed of peace across the land, trade restored to the world (or to Europe at least). A return to Beefeater's, White Horse and Calvert: the assurant glory of fine alcohol in the gold old US of A.

Those first four years in American had been a real education for Pedro Echevarria, a poor Bizkaian boy. Left as a herder for for months on end in the Independence and Ruby Mountains with only a .30-.30, and a dog for a friend he'd learned a lot more than he'd ever intended to. Long before the fancy rolling sheep wagons—summer and winter—a canvas tent for years had been his first American home. It was barely enough cover on the high mountain ranges to keep a man kicking and alive, but for four long years it had been his home. One thing the poor Bizkaian had learned if nothing else: Pedro Echevarria had learned to stockpile his food and supplies against all shortages, against all enemies.

Once upgraded to camp tender, he had learned to peddle his wares carefully: sometimes withholding favors, ferreting extras away to sell them later; sometimes dealing in black market what-you-have-asked-fors with the pitiable herders who were playing a poor hand, all desperate for a cup of sugar, a pound of flour— if only a kind word. ¡*Aie Ama!* A bota bag full of wine— the inner calf's skin lining giving it the fresh, musky flavor of flesh—gave visions of the young shepherdess Bernadette, *la Virgen de Arantzazú.*

By 1942 Pedro Echevarria was not a young man (maybe not even still middle-aged) who the hell knew? But as of yet there was no dirt in his teeth, as the old ones say: if it were up to Pedro, at sixty, he still had plenty left to prove. Like every natural leader there was plenty to say about him, and it seemed everyone at one time or another already had; nevertheless, fact was, Pedro Echevarria was nothing if not resilient. He knew he had his detractors, but he chalked that much up to envy. The joke among the Basques of Paradise (who made up about 50 percent of the total population) was that "Pete," aka: Peto, was a sheep in wolf's clothing. *Azeria solas ematen zaukanean ari, gogo emak heure oiloari.* (When speaking to the fox, keep an eye on your chickens!) To be fair to him and his operation, perhaps he was not even a wolf in a costume: just your garden variety wolf after all. They said he was a blind partner in the Nevada Hotel, but that was all on the QT. It was a well known fact that Pedro E was in on the campaign to legalize gaming in Paradise and throughout Nevada, but after the war that couldn't hurt.

As chief *hotelero* and downtown businessman, our Pedro and his Echevarria's was, after all, the cat's meow and pajamas. After the Roseanna Room at The Nevada had opened (maybe bad timing?) high tone folks like Ted Lewis and Bing Crosby preferred to take their evening meals (which irked Newt Crumley to no end) across the street at Echevarria's Hotel. Why, Peto was even able to consistently stock Death's Door Gin for Sophie Tucker's French 75 cocktails; and if lucky, Beefeater's for Dixie Lee Crosby (although in a pinch she'd drink pretty much anything to escape Bing). Echevarria's was a swanky joint for high-toned folk in cahoots with destiny, and Pedro Echevarria: *hotelier*, sheepman, miner and impresario, was still his ship's captain yet for a while until he wasn't as the war blew into 1942.

Elko Free Press, November 30, 1943

While participating in the landing at Papua, New Guinea, which began before dawn, we lost 37 LCI's before even reaching the beach. The men trying to get out of the landing crafts were killed by enemy mortar fire. Pete Zubieta of Elko was killed on the very first mission.
Joseph N. Corta Sgt. 542 Engineers Battalion

Citizen Support for America's G.I.s

"Wool is inherently non-flammable and won't melt in combat against the skin"

Elko Free Press, April 19, 1939

Shearing of sheep was started in Carlin on the 11th by Pete Elia. There are 11,000 sheep in the band and they belong to Pete Elia and the Gracian Eyroz estate. There are 35 men working with the sheep with 22 of them shearers, doing the work by hand. Elia estimates the average weight of the fleeces to be about nine pounds. Elia has recently finished shearing 7,000 sheep at Austin and the wool has been hauled to Carlin for later shipment. Most of the shearers are Mexican nationals.

Name	Rank	Status
Archibald, Vern E.	2 LT	KIA
Archuleta, Paul S.	PVT	KIA
Begay, Alfred	PVT	KIA
Begay, Taylor	PVT	KIA
Donique, Joe	PVT	KIA
Gabica, Joseph	PFC	KIA
Bill, Arbie	PFC	DNB
Dick, Glenn	PVT	DNB
Joe, Edward	PVT	KIA
Moon, Ray	PFC	KIA
Pete, Joe	PFC	KIA
Indart, Paul P.	CPL	DNB
Lague, Bruce	PFC	KIA
Olaeta, Laurence	PFC	KIA
Plaza, Joseph	2 LT	DNB
Garcia, Joe B.	PFC	KIA
Zubieta, Pete Jr.	PFC	KIA
Herrera, Jose	PFC	DNB
Lopez, Juan	PFC	DNB
Morales, Joe	SSC	KIA
Padilla, Roman	TECS	DNB
Raspaldo, Carlos E.	SSC	DNB
Torres-Melendez A.	PVT	DNB

Adrian Mariluch
KIA
U.S. Army
WWII

Arrascada bai zera, the name like a sidewinder sizzling alive on his tongue. From San Francisco, Lee checked the town rosters.

Long before the 8:15 had pulled into the station, Peto Echevarria reached the depot after pussyfooting his way across the Paradise tracks all the while fingering the knife in his pocket like his own member.

Who died, Basco? Where's the funeral? the painted lady in languid deshabille asked him at the dead-bolted door of Mona's D & D (Diddling & Dancing), her day just beginning.

Dana galdu, he calmly replied after taking another deep drag on the Lucky Strike he had just lit, then crushed it beneath the heel of his boot where the glowing fag died a fast death on the cold pavement.

Don't you speak English? Speak Christian goddamnit, man.

Gal-du. Da-na, this time more slowly. Hadn't she heard him the first time? Wasn't she listening?

Lost. Everything. Paradise Nevada.

Ura zan gizona, ura!

Zazpi oiñ ta erdi bai luze

> Goya
> Peto
> Belle
> Sally
> China Mary
> Black Betty
> Two-Time Tammy
> & Suzi Q

The Nevada

Now there was a man for you goddamnittohelly-oubetchya

It was Stella who let them in the locked door at the top of the fire escape of the Nevada Hotel. At last he held her finally tight against him, against time held her between the chinks of fate that had been their first imagining. Elias Eli Eleonora. Light from the neon sign NEVADA-NEVADA-NEVADA flashing wildly against them red-white *chiaroscuroed* in the clear dark against their bodies: this, his princess almost dancing, Leonora, he, Lee, absorbed by her warm harbor. It was she who this time knew the truth of now only. He who denied it his pockets flush with cash.

The world is too much with us late and soon. Hadn't he danced with her at The Golden just three years last May? Hadn't the war brought finally a fatalistic tolerance to everything once thought forbidden? If they danced together downstairs out in the open, would their hometown neighbors even care or discern whether the dashing serviceman in uniform was of

Chinese or Japanese ancestry? No matter. *Or konpon.* What the hell. Finally, when the joint was closing they sneaked downstairs and took their place on the floor. Then and there, they danced in the shadows of the Roseana Room. Danced for a golden moment for-evered: cheek-to-cheek all swing and sway to Sammy Kay. Bing crooning them near delirious to the moon. After midnight, she came to him upstairs, her in all her nakedness—in all her madness. Her scent left all over him. Leonora came to him dancing his aching desire, melted deliquesce all naked, her silk pongee dressing gown smelling of good scotch, sweet reckoning and Shalimar. Lee matched her every step.

And after again, it was she who knew the truth, but it made her reckless. She, who took his hand and pulled him dark inevitable into the sweet void wishing them their river full of stars full of stars at the end of shad-ows. Shaped by her, he stood and turned. She caught the sight of his smooth shoulders gold-bronze and beautifully square in the hotel mirror. His hips whis-pered the secret of her being, her only reason for living now this velvet half-light breathing him in. In her life she had never known anything as beautiful as his body not even the night sky. *Elise is pregnant, Leonora,* he told her. *Bennie's dead,* was all she said.

Even though most people in Paradise thought him still prominent (a rich man even), now all poor Peto dreamed of at night was food. On good nights, the great storehouses of Echevarria provided the scenario script-ing: hams, potatoes, *chorixuak*, the oaken barrels of fine California wine full to bursting against their staves. On other nights, it was just a poor shepherd's tale: a sack of flour, deer jerky, leg of old mutton. But of late, the old man in his dream world traveled as a starving Basque Lazarillo, a forest urchin foraging fields of *eusquel erria* the old Basque Country: dreaming of half-rotted cabbages, *setak* wild mushrooms and forgotten carrots— one night he'd found a fat chestnut and scored it with his knife!

> *Ai-ta* ... Father.
> *Pu-ta* whore

(*Nora zoaz, gixontxu?* Where to my little man?)

And all the while—all these years long, he'd had the knife with him, kept the hard-fashioned tool of fine Spanish steel at the ready. Allegedly it was a knife from Toledo: a sailor's knife, an adventurer's knife, the knife of a New World conquistador. Forged or not in the land of La Mancha, in this America for this Amadís de Gaula, it was his Tizona: Protector and Avenger, potato dicer, onion slicer, flesh divider, piercer and pike. Whether facing the badge of the law or the axe-handled faces of crack buckaroos, Peto was Knight of the Green Knife. (Granted, that time up to the Spanish Ranch at Tuscarora there'd been all that blood, but with no one the wiser.) For over thirty years Pedro Echevarria had had no other real American trouble. Nothing he couldn't deal with—up until now.

Round these parts they say it takes a whole lot of pluck and a mighty steady hand for a man to slit his own throat with a pocket knife—near impossible. But being Basque, Pedro Echevarria finally got er done.

The fishin and the fuckin, that much he'd miss.

1952
Pauline

As early as the early 1950s casino owner-politician Paul Elcano had made critical political connections with racketeer Danny Rose, owner of Elko's famous Nevada Hotel, as well as to Las Vegas mobster, Sam Gianncano. The actual link between them remains a mystery. *A Political History of Nevada*, Robert Kelly: Reno (University of Nevada Press, 2005) p. 15

I served Mr. Rose for forty years. I was his personal secretary and hostess. I did a lot of things for him. Most folks in town know me first from Echevarria's. Then I was dining room hostess at the the Roseanna Room. That was always the swankest place in town in the forties and fifties. It's where Mr. Rose started bringing in big name entertainment. You know, them big bands: Sophie Tucker, Sammy Kaye. Wayne Newton was just a boy here when he got his start in Paradise, Ted Lewis, way before Vegas. That was before these mines brought in the riff and the raff. Just a different kinda folk back then. The stars were all here: Bing Crosby, Jimmy Stewart, Maureen O'Hara, Gypsy Rose Lee, you name it. *Would you like to swing on a star? Carry moonbeams home in a jar? Heaven, I'm in heaven, and my heart beats to that I can hardly speak* . . .

Some pretty high-toned people came through those doors: Pat McCarran, Guvnor Elcano, Guvnor Salter, all the politicians and casino owners. Why, one year Mr. Rose made Mr. Bing Crosby honorary mayor with a big white ten-gallon hat and we had all a Hollywood out to the ranch. I still got the clippin from *The Free Press*. Levis company made him a denim tuxedo and at the fair all the starlets had a calf ropin contest with all the publicity folks. The photos are still up in The Brand Room downstairs. Paradise has always been some kinda slap-happy rip-roaring place!

Whozat? Senator Bible? Why, he aways ate right at my station. I think he passed out due to high blood pressure, but gossipy folk said he was dead drunk. I always served him. I would know now, wouldn't I? O'Connor? As Irish as Paddy's pig. I'm Irish too, partly I think. He was a fine-lookin man, but missin one leg cause he was a war hero an all. To tell you the truth it wasn so odd really, just kinda stumpy. Frank Sinatra, now there was a man. Usually I didn't take too much to them I-talians. They was hard to get out of the dining room after closin, just like them Basco boys when they started singin about the old country you couldn't get rid of em— at least them I-talians tipped good! Mr. Rose had Cuban cigars imported special. Sometimes one of em would get interested in the girls, but I don know, seemed their attention was more on the singin or something, kinda peculiar.

Now that Jimmy Stewart was a real gentleman.
The only star I ever met that was even better in person. Just like that Mr. Smith goes to Washington or that guy that dies and comes back in "It's a Wonderful Life," but that wife a his was a real bitch-kitty, pardon my French. I had to put on my sweet smile swinette to stomach that one. They bought a big ranch out to Thousand Springs, had a Venetian glass tile swimming pool and a screening room and all special foods flown in and Mr. Stewart she ran him around like a lap dog. Strange what some folks want. Mr. Stewart had the longest fingers ya know, real elegant like a piana player's. There was some nasty rumors floatin round, but they just ain true. Never once in all those years did he visit the houses. Honest to God, never even acted interested in women. Gloria, that was her name: Glory Glory Hallelujah! She never let him drink and her endin up an alkie n all.

Mr. Rose? What didja wanna know about Mr. Rose? Nothing too unusual. Everbody's got their little quirks. He liked his—Oh politics, I don know that much about politics. You said you were a historian, dinchya now? You wan the truth. I don know much about that. No, I never saw him in Carson City. Oney time I was in Cartoon City was in the late '50s. I was nurse companion to Representative Robertson. Hell no I never had no formal nurse's training, but he wasn really sick either, ya know? Mosly his wife's Daddy an the rest a them nice Democrats wantin to keep him off the Assembly floor. We had a chauffeured limousine every morning from Reno. I never was sure why we just didn jus stay in Carson. She ended up in Sparks, ya know, at the nut house. Swallowed a whole bottle a Lysol once. Hysterical type, female troubles an no kids. Men don hang round that type long unless they got money and their

Daddy's got money and her Daddy had money. Got
the ole boy into the legislature: he owed him big time.
The Guvnor? Oh, then he was only senator, a Basco real
good-lookin fella, a real politico. He was in casinos or
somethin in Reno and Vegas. They was all tangled up
with the casinos back then. Thas how Mr. Rose knew
so many big shots, helped em out a lot if ya know what
I mean. The Guvnor was a smooth man, real controlled,
ya know? He was a real Donde Gente. The kind a man
tha looks back at his shoulder muscles in the mirror.
He sure had nice shoulders!

Yeah, I met Mr. Hughes, a real queer duck that one,
but they said he was real intelligent, an airplane engineer or somethin. He was with Kate Hepburn back
then, and tha wasn no public knowledge neither. Now
there was a real star! He flew Miss Hepburn out here
one time during deer season. They come into town all
stylin with blue and red Hudson Bay jackets all check-
er boarded up and Stetson hats, ya know, hand-tooled
leather boots all too new. A course everyone knows
she was really with Spencer Tracy, but his wife was a
Catholic. No divorce, ya know. Come again? I heard he
gave him some money for the campaign. Oh, in the 60s
sometime. I don't remember exactly what year, but
that would be your department now, wouldn it? Mr.
Hughes never carried money, if you were with him
they said you better be prepared to pay. And he even
poneyed up the dough for the college! Strange with all
that money he never actually handled money, thought
it was unsanitary or somethin. That ain all he thought
was unsanitary.

No, I don rightly know. Maybe he was in on the
deal. Didjya know I got a screen test? I was gonna be a
star. A friend of Mr. Hughes set it up, but nothin came

of it, not that I was really expectin anything. He said I
had it, ya know? I think it was just the tits. I woulda
liked to have made it though, just to bring my family outa California and set em up nice in a Hollywood
bun-ga-low, but Mama was already gone by the time
Mr. Rose discovered me. Who's really "got it made"?
Ever think about that? Take my Pauline, for example.
Real nice kids, nice house, lotsa dough, ya know? Her
husband, well, I'd never tell her. They don have much
to do with me anyway which is fine. It's a different
world other side a the tracks, ain it? Those from that
side a the hill can sure as hell come cross our side and
then lickity-split back again, but we don dare cross the
line now do we? I don blame em though. Glad she made
it across. It took everything I had. That husband a hers
thinks his shit don't stink: that he's a regular Marques
de Buglos or somethin, ya now? It's all theater, ya ask
me. *All the men merely players*, that's Shakespeare. Boy,
aren't they though!

Huh? Oh thas right—Mr. Rose. I practically lived
with him for thirty years and I cain tell you I knew the
man. There's people like that, kinda like actors in their
own play. I don know much about his past really either,
left some troubles back East or somethin. No, she was
his second wife: sickly, female troubles lotsa female
troubles. She was a church lady though, maybe not her
fault. They all get female trouble they not usin it regular. Whazat now? Yeah, they had some kids, shipped
em all back East to boarding school. Mr. Rose and his
wife would fly out to vacation somewhere during the
holidays less somethin was up here.

Why, one Valentine's Day Mr. Rose calls up the
florist, Fred Jackson, to order two dozen yellow roses
sent up to the apartment. He called me that, his yellow

rose a Texas which is peculiar since I'm from Arkansas.
Well, ole Fred Jackson had a sense a humor if nothin
else. He asked Mr. Rose on the phone if he also wanted
two dozen red roses sent to Mrs. Rose too when she returned from Palm Springs and tha was when the town
was still on a party line. Everbody in town knew come
ever Valentine's Mr. Rose was out four dozen roses!
Ha! Them wives are the first to know, ya ask me.
Come again? How the hell do I know? Echevarria's
was always fulla politicians. They gotta eat like the
resta us. What? Why, Mr. Rose aways paid a course, it
was his place for a time, ya know. Hell, if I know *why*.
Hey, not to hurt your feelins or anything, but I think
politics are just plain borin. I never understood what
all the fuss was about. I guess it comes down to power
and usually the me wannee kind. Politicians talk more,
drink more, screw more and dress better than the resta
us, but the truth is they're jus folks who gotta sit to shit
too. They just got somethin itchin in em tha makes em
try harder to convince themselves that they're just
o.k., ya know?

Take my Pauline for example. Pauline's on the city
council, school board, I don know what all else, probably
be mayor. A course no one says nothin cause Marshall,
thas her husband (what kinda fag name is that anyways?), he's a judge. Pauline went to law school too,
oney she gave it up for his career and the kids and to
git her hair done. She mosely plays golf and goes shop-
pin. She's got it all, I guess. They both helped with the
money, ya know? I made damn sure she never had to be
a workin girl: finishin school in San Francisco, design-
er clothes, college, e-lo-cu-tion lessons, summers back
East. She's what I could never be. It ain her fault I am
what I am. She cain help it. Everyone in Paradise knows

where she come from, but she pretends they don so it's awright. Life is all what you see, young man. Not out there, up here in the noggin. (For men it's a little lower mosta the time).

Whazat? Where did I meet him? Mr. Rose or Guvnor Elcano? It was through Mr. Giancanno. I'd left home real young and had a friend in Reno said she could git me a job slingin hash since I looked older than I was. I was aways what you might call, *well-endowed*— big tits, ya know? Too bad you couldn see me back then. Why, Mr. Rose said once said it wasn that I was fat it was jus that my belly had caught up to my chest kicked in by my ass. Ain that funny though? He was a real joker, tha Danny Rose!

Anyways, I was in this club by the Mapes on Virginia Street in Reno an I wasn more'n fifteen, but they gave me a job anyways doin dishes, whatever there was. Mama had the three little ones still back home an Daddy never found steady work again after the accident. I done it on my own decision, wasn nobody pushin me out. We got choices in life—everbody forgets that. Ever day of our lives we can choose. I was poor and low class and my people was dependin on me for a livin. I didn have no education and now higher folks can look their noses down on me and judge? Too bad for them. It's a near impossible proposition for them higher folks to get some perspective, ya know? They don have to move outa their comfort and the resta us is invisible: niggas n messicans, poh white trash, the Chinese n all the goddamned immigrants. Fact is, that's most of us.

I coulda slung hash or cleaned toilets now couldn I now? Why, those boys a Pauline's and Mr. Sonofabitch don even have a clue what it's like to live back in my day, an it's a right good thing ask me. Devil din make me do nothin, Mister. Devil's here in us thas all. We's the devil an the angel all at once. I made the choices, but I tried to be good to folks aways. I tried hard to understand em. Most wicked things come from just not seein people. Ya gotta understand all their fears, look their pain right dead in the eye before you really know em. After that, goddamnit, ya gotta forgive em! It's a tall order, Mister.

My Mama died real young. She was only thirty-five and she never knew about me in Reno—where the money come from I sent em. I got mine too now, didn I? Exploited? Isn that what you young people call it nowadays? We called it goddamn survival. My personal opinion is that mos men ain got no power anyways. Thas why they's aways struttin round like banty roosters, cocks-a-the-walks. Damn I'm glad I wasn no man. Ya wanna know a secret? The diddlin thing, it's the man who's admirin himself through all the romance, ya know? Men never court ladies or even try to please em really. Like the tango, he's got all the forward moves. Those Don Juan ladies' man types are the most pitiful. You wouldn think that now, would you? They're woman haters. What they wan is to admire themselves through you. Thas what they teach the girls young—when you're jus startin out in the business. Praise, praise, praise and more praise. Honey what a big . . . Baby, you're the best . . . Oh you make me crazy! You, you you you! Ain no different with husbands oney when you're a whore like that you sold yourself out to get paid. The wives, they owned full-time. They don choose. They don get paid.

Ya know a Chinaman once told me, the Chinaman said, "Confucius say, *Be careful what you ask for: You might get it awright.*" Back then I thought tha was the mos crazy-assed thing I'd ever heard. Now, I know it's the gods' truth. It's not getting what ya want tha counts, it's wantin what you have that makes ya rich. I feel like a goddamn millionaire lately (I guess thas not so much nowadays, huh?). I don have no regrets. I made my choices like anybody. I don know much. I'm not ejucated like y'all. I never read much but I listened. I really listened to folks. I learned that from Mama, she was a good listener. It's the truest way of lovin someone, ya know? To see em there as they really are and still love em for it. It's deep in all the myths and poetry. In all those Ippanishads and the Bagagadavida and all over the place. I did ok on the first three, it's thet judging and envyin that really gets ya. I coulda done better on that. Why if I had another life I would learn all the languages if I could. Pauline speaks Spanish and French. Can you imagine anything finer than speaking to someone in their own language? Othewise we're just all Babelin foreigners. Words are the greatest gift of the gods, donchya think? An the greatest curse. We need to be right careful with the words we use, at least that's what I think.

Thank ye Jesus Lord, Thy tender mercies. I'm not the church religious type, but I know about God. At first, I gave lotsa money to the church. Now they won put me in the Catholic cemetery. The Presbyterians don want me neither. I was a harlot and a sinner I guess. What's a harlot anyways? There's lots of em in the Bible and they're all around Jesus so it's confusing. I wonder if it ever matters in the accountin of it if you're the bugger doin it or the one bein done to? I'm not worried for myself, but Pauline and Mr. Sonafabitch are gonna have to do it—the buryin I mean. That makes a big problem for em. I don want to make no embarrassment. I know who I am, ya know, like Socrates. Trouble is whole town knows me too! It don seem to matter quite as much out West. Ya know, John Wayne movies and Miss Kitty n all. What was up with those two anyways? That Little Joe with the squatty hat ever git a girlfriend on Bonanza? I dunno. Truth is we all gotta catch the bus west in the end now any way. Don we? *Swing low, sweet chariot, comin for to carry me hooo-ome . . . swing low sweet chariot . . . Sometimes I feel like a motherless child . . . comin for to carry me ho-ome . . .*

Shit. I musta dropped off to sleep, lullabied my damn self to sleep, ha! Ain that a hoot? Dyin must sound all kinda melancholy to you, but it ain atall. It's just our homecomin. Our people are there; they been here all along. Most a the end here is all a rerememberin—the taste of a warm summer strawberry picked from the patch when you was six, the smell a your Mama's arm, that gold yeller light on the snow in winter that somehow turns pink. There's somethin about the stars too, light years and time relative. By the time their light reaches us they're all dead an gone. Thas like our lives. I don say it's right, but it feels true. A star has a half life. There's a glowin after the light is gone, a trace that stays. I wasn even sad when I lost him, an I was expectin to be cause we knew aforehand, ya know. Some other specialists said it was cancer: his breath eaten all away by maggots in his chest. Thas what got Daddy too, the black lung eventual. Maybe he came out West for the climate anyways, an those folks a his was wrong. They eighty-sixed him right outa the casinos, said he was a card counter. He never cheated though, just beat em at their own crooked games. After, it was like it had all been a dream an I couldn remember the plot much less the main characters. Who was I? Who was he? What does it all matter when you cash in all your chips anyways? All that eatin n talkin; thinkin n fuckin all wrapped up like a Christmas package in a casket. They put him in a silk suit, crammed his whole life into a goddamn mahogany box with silver handles. None of his high fallutin bunch even came. I was the only one there besides Mrs. Echevarria, Digger Brown, the two queers from The Ritz, Lee the Chinaman and that Basco tha was his friend. You know, the one they call Indian-o.

There's clearness ya get out a holdin death all close like that. Clean with patches a light from the other side. *Through a glass darkly*, he'd a said. I got pieces of it before, but I could never hold on to it for good, just patches. You ever been with the dead, son? Oh, I know how it seems, but to tell the truth it don spook me none, it's comfortin. I seen Mama coupla a nights ago and she was smooth n lovely as a girl: all that strawberry gold hair and she was wearin a cotton dress all fresh dried from the sun. My hair was like hers oney it went dark on me after I was a girl, then I touched it up again now it's gone white like I took some kinda bad fright! Why when I was a girl my Mama smelled sweet fresh from heaven like just baked bread. I reckon thas what it must be like when ya get there to be with them again. All young skin gone warm again in the sun, the smell a new grass round a spring, the sunset burned down all gold into silver ash—

Paul Elcano? Hell if I know. The prize fight? I guess so. It was a pretty big fight in Reno, I think. An Injun kid from up Owyhee way. Everbody thought he'd make the Olympics. Mr. Rose was only tryin to give him a break, make some dough. Those people are poor like us, ya know, Paiute n Shoshoni. *Newe,* they call themselves "the people". *Squirrel-eaters* is what we call em. *Dai-bo* outsider is wha they call us. I reckon they got that right. Oh I dunno, a lota people had a line out. Yeah? So maybe he did. A lotta money was changin hands in the back room. That Injun kid Jackie Woods was a real respectful boy, truth be known, not much older'n seventeen, used to order two pieces a cherry pie at the counter, coffee with extra cream if I recall. He threw that fight, they said, later got killed in a car wreck in Owyhee canyon. Ole man Tremewan fished him out. Shame, they like their whiskey when they can get it awright. Damn fine fighters though. Quiet folk. I think they know something.

Look here fella, I tole you I don know nothin bout nobody important. You ain the first to come sniffin round like a dog lookin for a piece, ya know. There's aways been pleny a rumors bout Mr. Rose and Paul Elcano. It's all pure envy, you ask me. Whazat now? Was I ever in love? Ha! Thas a good one. Honey, thas not my business—persuasion is. There was one. You kinda put me in minda him. He wrote some books too. He was real intelligent. A thinkin man, intense, ya know? The kinda man thas gota brushfire a blazin in his head—tha cool cold starlight burnin. A magma n titanium all at once, ya know? When I was jus startin out one ole gal told me you could always tell by their hands, but I knew it through their eyes. Is jus somethin in there, glowin urgent like it had breath. Somethin tryin so hard to get out at you a man'd die tryin. Wanna know the truth? You do?

Thas what I really did it for, not later for the money or the things I got. I hated men to buy me presents. After a while I didn need no money anyways. I could stand on my own pretty soon awright. I'll tell you one big secret, young man, then you can go tell all your modern book friends. I lived my whole life to see what was on the other side a that man's eyes, to stand there full in my power and see em come to me, a beggin an a cryin, reachin out like babies wan it, wan me so bad. You ever wan it that bad, son? Anybody your age ever wan it that bad? What you callin it now, the "sexual revolution"? "women's lib"? Some liberation. Whadaya do now? Just screw whenever ya wan whoever ya wan or what? It ain even really about sex if ya wanna know the truth. It's about *Desire*—the life force Eros pushin out of us beyond and through: why, it's Creation, God. *Sehnsucht.* The mystery's all the thing, whas between a man an a woman: it's the only story there ever is. It's what holds us all together and pulls us all apart. It's the wishin n waitin, the hopin it's the real thing this one this time. It's not holdin on to it or havin it forever. You might as well catch a star by the tail. It's jus one long moment happened between just you two before you catch your breath and all time stops. A minute a paradise before he touches you, before you're a touchin him. It's the touchin, like we'd had a shot at heaven, a chance to practice a little with God before we blow all dead out. He studied e-lect-tro-lumen-essence or something like that. He was brilliant in a real hurtin kinda way.

Come again? No, not right off. When he first brought me to town we had the apartment, oney one I ever had. This room too in the hotel so folks wouldn talk. Funny, I never owned a place a my own, maybe none of us do really. I coulda afforded it too, but I never seemed to belong to anyone or a house. Thas why I never smoked—it's actually against hotel rules. Thing is nobody pays no never mind to the rules. I always liked my room anyways and the apartment was real elegant, ya know, a "penthouse" they call it. I wonder why they called it that? Maybe ya get all pent up in it or something. No, he never came here. It was all mine. I suppose so, yeah. He gave me lotsa things if thas what ya mean. You the IRS or what, Mister? Men were always givin me things. Lota good it does us in the end. I pawned all the jewelry before I got to this point anyways. Lost my taste for that kinda thing a long time ago. Whazat? Oh, I know what they say about leavin Pauline outa the will 'n all, but it wasn exactly, uh, fittin, if ya know what I mean. He did awright by us. They both did.

I managed awright. I jus kept on workin up to the end. I aways liked it downstairs better anyways. Worked up until a few years ago, that when the diabetes took the feelin outa my feet an I couldn stand through a whole shift. It wasn fair for the others to pick up my slack. I enjoyed real workin anyways. I ain got no regrets. I do somethin cause I want to. But, believe you me, I didn get to that point until later in life— much later. Youth is wasted on the young, donchya think, young man? Why, a course ya don't. Mosta this life we's just grasping. I dunno.

Anyways back to the real story. That first night we never did nothing really, ya know. Oney he touched me where nobody had before. In the center somewhere I never knew existed. Maybe it wasn him doin the touchin atall. At first, I thought maybe there was somethin wrong with me, ya know? I was afraid he'd tell Mr. Rose I wasn, you know, *good*. We got over that awright. Did we ever! Why once round Christmas, special cause he usually only came out West in the summertime after his university was over, we was parked in a seedan up out on Pyramid in a goddamned blizzard an we didn even know the worst of it yet—-we'd run out of gas! *Mehr licht! Meine Gott, mehr licht!* he'd said. (That must be 'outa gas' in German) and then he sat there and laughed his head off like a looney. Out there on the high desert plateau twenty miles from town! We was in a pickle awright, naked as jaybirds in the dead a winter and the heater long gone. The doctors said he had TB, consumption they used to call it. The cold musta blasted it outa him up there that time cause he lived on still. My Mama died of the consumption. It wasn uncommon like polio back then only I hear they've got that one near licked.

I wonder where all the words go when our light's gone down here? You ever thoughta that? They bury you in the dirt and all thas left is your name and a few numbers on that cold hard stone. I really don talk to too many folks no more. This hip's all gone and I cain get downstairs easy. Say, I was wondrin if I could get your advice on something I been chewin on lately. Awright then, much obliged. I was wondrin what name you think I oughta put on, you know, *my stone?* So Pauline will remember mainly. I wan a pretty one now: a nice, pink marble one like that undertaker's wife in Wells got after that bad car wreck. Nothin real fancy, mind ya, jus like decent folk, ya know? I done wan no funeral, only the name part seems important. It's not like my people are round these parts anyways. They're probly all gone wherever they are.

I been thinkin. What does a family name matter in heaven? Does it really matter if Pauline's Rose or Elcano? A darn sight better'n Malasechevarria Guericabeitia ya ask me. Even if he has her run for office? Are we all there together then, mister? I think so: yes, that'd be right nice. I been thinkin, well, how about Estela? Thas right, the Spanish way cause a Mr. Hughes' movie n all. I aways liked the Latins, passion *corazón*. Them Bascos are Spanish some of em in the Pyrenees oney they'll tell ya they ain. It's all so warm n colored an Picasso there I imagine. Goya and the stars. It's hot there mosley too, all that desert in the middle. Meo Cid n Salamanca Burgos La Escorial Valladolid, such purdy words ain they? I always fancied myself Spanish. "*Estela*," thas all, on the stone I mean. I think I'd to name myself in the end. *Stela* a marker like a star. And like an ancient mariner I can guide myself to him, up there in the galaxy.

Why, Mister, we'd set up there above town parked in the foothills for hours jus settin, jus dreamin. Sometimes I'd try to count the stars lookin up at The Rubies and he'd laugh! He'd tell me old stories about the sky gods and goddesses of the earth, the way they all got it on: Ursus, Apollo, Zeus and Astarte; Amaya, Venus, Jupiter and Thor, Ariadne n Pandora Minerva Demeter Prometheus. Such great fun! Oncet while he was lookin deep into thos stars a his all of a sudden he up n aks me, *Stella? Do you know what a half life is?* Why, I tell you, my heart just plumb stopped like a lead ball in my chest. Like I'm sposed to really know something scientific. He was an astro-physicist or something. It made me feel real bad cause I was wishin then I could be one a them ejucated ladies n go back East with him to live and talk to him about all his discoveries forever and a day. *Stella, I only lived a half life till you,* all poetical like. Tha was what stopped me. I'll never forget it. Kinda sounded like a Perry Como tune, I dunno, it was more. Right then how could I know he was dyin? Would I a done anything different then with the knowing?

When he said that I kept on sobbin like all the hurt

in me had come up and gushed out all at once like. And what does he do but takes me real gently up in his arms like I was made a porcelain like that Pietà or somethin. And what if he doesn start rockin me back and forth and back again like ya would a babe lookin all the time deep down into my eyes: *Io son ventuo al pinto de la rota/one Iorizzonte, quando il sol corca,/ci partorisce il geminato cielo* . . . An I don rightly know what he's sayin, but I understand beyond the words through the sound a his voice and his chest movin up and down just breathin in a rhythm. None a the crap no more. I could let it all go. It was all light together, all colors swirlin in a prism. You ever seen the colors a the sunset over the high desert? Away from your city life I mean. You got too much electricity now, son. It ain the same. If I had time I'd take you up to Adobe Summit on the full moon—maybe a milk moon, a mother's moon the one before summer to see the night stars. *You'd like that.* But I. .m ru nin ou ta air her uh outa air here. You move my machine over a bit will ya so I can check the ox y gen a gin?

Much better, now I can breathe. The first time he drove me up there the radio was on and it's Nat King Cole and we're sittin in that red convertible a his lookin up at the stars and I'm waitin, ya know, for his hand on me or somethin and after it wasn comin really wantin it to come then, ya know? I'd put on fresh drawers and Evening in Paris (you know the kind in the deep blue bottle like the night sky) an I'd jus had my hair done, so what gives? There we are sittin up there on the hill and he's bought my dinner down at Echevarria's and all he can do is hold me in his arms an look up at all these goddamned crispy stars like buckaroo camp fires lit all over the sky, and I start to thinkin he's, well, a little off, right peculiar. Then I start lookin at em myself.

What else am I sposed to do? They said he was a remittance man from back East. He'd had some big trouble too—I don know. Thas generally why folks get a mind to come out West, either they got no money or some trouble or disappointment back where they came from like in all those westerns. It's true! I think he mighta, you know, how do you say it nowadays? I think he liked men, too. Maybe that was it. He wrote a book of poetry that was published, maybe in Polish or Czechoslavakian. I can never keep all those easterns straight, can you? I woulda liked to seen that, then I'da known a real poet, ya know. That first summer he was out here figurin out how to measure up light (at least thas what he said). At night we'd drive up to the foothills above town out by the dump. Thas why he came to Nevada in the first place, cause the sky was so clear you could aways see the stars. Isn that funny now? They were so *crisp*, so *scintillate*, he said. Why, I can hear him say that like he was sittin right here beside me. Ya know somethin, young man? Maybe he was a real poet much as he doted on words. He plain lingered over em, catchin the consonants on his tongue like honey, roundin em out over the low long vowels. Why he'd make em up into words like a lonesome man making love to himself. He had a way a turnin a phrase, that one. Why, he was a reglar philosopher too, that Zolton. A mystic if there ever was one. It was odd. As smart as he was he aways said it was me had all the answers. *Stella, Estella d'amour ci sta remota...*

Wha? Where's my manners? A political history of Nevada, you say. I don't believe I caught your name. Robert Kelly, that has a nice ring to it. Not "Rob" or "Bob, but "Robert". I like it! I shall call you "*Rober*" the way the French say it without the t' on the end a it. Sor-

ry I couldn help you that much. I don't know the real
history, just gossip and bits and snippets of things. Are
you anybody famous? Anybody important by chance?
No? well don't let it worry you none. Me neither.

Uh, one more thing, before I go if you've got time
I mean. *Monsieur Rober? Je desirais s'il vous plait* (that
means "I would desire…"), *Je desirais* one a them señor-
ita peasant blouses, ya know, like Jane Russell spilled
her boobs outa in "The Outlaw" for the funeral (Oh no.
No funeral. What was I thinking?) Just a moment of silence and a prayer if you know one. But don't forget the
blouse *s'il vous plait*. The one with embroidry an pully
strings in "The Outlaw". I still got big tits even though
they're on the southerly side now. An I'd like a skirt
with clean, lacy petticoats all around, lotsa petticoats
like Scarlet O'Hara in "Gone With the Wind". Them
skirts full bright painted colorful like Messican girls in
the Westerns wear with sandals, some soft camel hide
sandals like them Marys in the desert round Jesus.
That'd be right nice.

Et Monsieur Rober? You be my last man and maybe
you could read a nice po-em out for me at the gravesite
like he would. One a them sonnets by that I-talian in
tha Renaissance business. Whaz his name anyways?
Petraca? Petrarch, thazit with that Laura gal. Aways in
the end in the movies all ya wanna know is: Did that
fella ever get his girl or what? Did she really love him?
Was it all real? Tell em in Stella's story he did and she
did an it came out fine and Pauline's happy. A good girl
and awright. Tell her I love her. She's all I could never
be.

The widespread speculation that the affair between the alleged "Dark Lady" (who may have,

in fact, at times been quite fair) and JFK who was connected through Gianncano and Rose to Elcano in Nevada is largely unsubstantiated. Like the muse of Shakespeare's sonnets, or the historical reality of Petrarch's Laura, the true identity of the star witness for the prosecution (the Divine Feminine, if you will) to this day remains uncertain: a mystery encrypted in the annals of private life, her identity belongs to the domain of fiction, not to that of true history.
A Political History of Nevada, Robert Kelly: Reno (University Nevada Press, 2005).

. . . e la stella d'amor ce sta remota/ per lo raggio
    lucent
che la entorca/si di traverse che le si ta velo.

1962
URRE TA
VIZCAYA

Eskual Herritik jin nintzan / I came from the
Basque Country in 1963 / *hiru hogeita hiruan
neguko lanbete inguruan* / when winter chores
were at their peak / *urtarrilaren hiruan* / on
the third day of January / *Geroztik hunat sortu
lekua beti atxiki dut gouan,* / Ever since then I
have always had my birthplace in mind / *Berrriz
sortu behar nuela* / And then I realized that here
I must be born again. Gratian Alfaro

Elko Daily Free Press, May 28, 1965

Two bars of gold, valued at $82,000,
were on this morning's United Air-
lines flight, destined for further
refinement and recasting at the Federal Mint. They were the first two
bars of full-production from the
Carlin Gold Mine poured yesterday by
Plato Malozemoff, president of New-
mont Mining Corp., owner of the mine.

For the last time, Joxe Unamuno walked up the steep curving S that led from the salt estuaries of the Cantabrian to the medieval village of Itziar along the Pilgrim's Way. The tang of fresh cut grass was on his tongue, he sucked it in like oxygen. Before taking his vows on Tuesday he pledged one final pilgrimage to the Cave of Ekain to seek favor and blessing of Mari of Amboto. By late afternoon, he would return to the stone gothic church of Itziar moored like a ship to the precipitous green hills of Euskadi, return there to pray to *Nuestra Señora* and the Virgin (who was one and the same difference) for safe voyage. His bag was packed, his passage indentured. Tomorrow he would be in America. Sweet Promised Land.

Cocorico! The old rooster of Txerturi Goikoa heralded his early coming, always remembering the boy.

Cucurrucu cu cu! The mourning doves of Laztana farmstead bid him good morning (not knowing that they bid him *adieu*).

Ironically enough, this moonstruck priest-to-be Basque who had little acumen for the pastoral life, was now destined to become "*Pastor de los Pastores*", Father Joe of Paradise, Nevada, good shepherd to all the good shepherds 1962.

Baaaaaa aaaaa!

At least sheep speak a universal language, he thought to himself before leaving the *baserri. Or do they?* This much was certain: Joxe Unamuno was fresh off the farm, Santa Maria de Etxeberria, newly minted from the seminary.

> The Silver State, July 17, 1894
> An insane Basque sheepherder was ar-
> rested yesterday morning and locked
> up. He was wandering around town car-
> rying a shepherd dog on his back, and
> is supposed to have packed the animal
> all the way from the sheep camp where
> he was employed, about 40 miles south
> of here. His insanity seems to be of a
> religious turn, as since put in jail
> he spends most of his time muttering
> prayers, interspersed with howls al-
> most hideous enough to scare a rail-
> road "scab" into being a gentleman.

Father Joe

My, that cowgirl was tall.

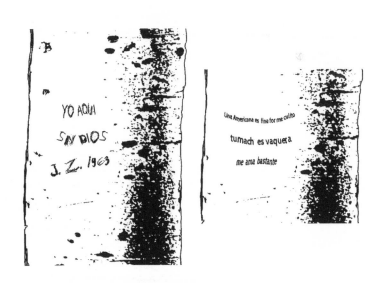

In Bilbao city, over too many whiskeys before leaving, Pete Echeverria—who'd spent twenty-eight years between Buffalo and Boise—briefed his great nephew on the journey to Nevada with many tall tales, *"No ho-houses too spensive clean you feets good (foots rot) and forgit de goddamaned Amerikano prepositions! You never gettin dem, anyways no how, mutiko!"* Also providing him at the time with connections in New York and Ogden (the wrong railway spur). Trouble was "Tío Peech" hadn't been in America for thirty years (since 1932) and Joxe was hell bent for leather, bound for Nevada. (Even a young Basque seminarian knew Buffalo was in Wyoming). No matter, the arch-diocese in New York had also given him the name of another Father Joe (Larrañaga) who had just taken up residence at the Church of St. James, 32 James St. in Manhattan. *Biar*, tomorrow he was bound for Paradise via New York City. Tomorrow he'd be flying! Today he had one hell of a hangover.

Valentin Aguirre Travel Agency

82 Bank Street   New York, N. Y. 10014

AL SERVICIO DE LA COLONIA ESPAÑOLA
DESDE EL AÑO 1910
Teléfono   Cable:
Chelsea 3-2705   "Aguirre"

After hailing a cab in New York (*¡ostias!*), Father Joe Unamuno exchanged money on Broadway and ate his first bagel with a piss water cup of "coffee." Still famished, he bought two kosher hot *dogs*? with German mustard, and sauerkraut (*¡ostias!*). After fine dining out on the sidewalk, a grimy panhandler shoved him to the curb for the delay in his English and a handout: Joxe felt like jumping ship right then and there. Caravaggio!

he noticed was at The Metropolitan. *Death of the Virgin!* He'd arrived like Dante to his Paradiso, his city on a hill, but all he wanted now was to miss the bus to the real Paradise, "Neeybaaada," as the old Indianos in Bilbao called the place.

On one of the street corners bracketing the American Museum of Natural History and the Met, *Tristan und Isolde!* He quickly devised American Joe's Master Plan #2: he would telegraph the archbishop's office (like in a 30s black-and-white-movie) and tell the church to forget it (thanks very *mucho* for the solid Jesuit education); thereafter, he would go to live among animals in the forests and cafés of Manhattan. He would listen there forever to the voiceless voices in vast canyons of concrete, of glass, sing arias with pigeons *coo coo* (there were a lot of pigeons) at the Metropolitan and pitch his shepherd's tent to paint ballerinas *à la Dégas. Aie ama,* I am just a poor boy from Gipuzkoa. What bad luck this to reach the shores of the Promised Land and have to leave the shore. *¡Pobre de mí!*

It was no less than the magnificent vision of the Continental Divide, after hours of cramped flight on the DC-3, which finally got to him: New World indeed. He was gob-smacked by the scope and extension of the Western landscape: the Rockies, the Uintas, then that prophetical emptiness of the Great Salt Lake, the Great Basin! *This is the place,* Brigham Young the scion of Zion and brave new polygamist, a century ago had decreed. Brave new world, indeed.

From this eagle's eye view, the topography of Nevada looked as if the gods had shaken out some Olympian horse blanket, setting it down as it rippled into over a hundred mountain ranges north to south. There were very few towns, much less cities, beyond Denver, but in the emptiness there was beauty—such grandeur not his dreams had seen. At the tops of mountain ranges which scratched the sky at twelve to fourteen thousand feet, Father Joe could discern the tree line demarcations between the lower vegetation and higher bald granite and scree along which the antediluvian bristlecone grew. (It was stunning.) Below the great fingerling draws of mahogany, spruce, aspens and pine. The high desert plateaus between the high mountain ranges made the priest think of an Old Testament God, some great chthonian triumph of His interface with the tribes of Israel and Abraham. *This is the place. Apoteosi di Sant'Ignazio.* The mountains of the West were like great painting. They were Old Testament scripture.

Ad majorem Dei Gloriam.

When the plane made landfall, Father Joe took in a sky brilliant as Venetian glass over the dust town outpost. (Was it the altitude or was his brain starved for oxygen?) After some time waiting there on the sticky tarmac, it appeared as if no one had come to meet him after all. In the near distance he could see the gaudy little cow town—all cowboy bar, dust and casino neon. With yet another sigh of deep regret, he took it upon himself (with faith and conviction) to look up from the outskirt fringes of Paradise, Nevada (praying for strength or some kind of sign?) and saw there before him in the distance the jagged towers of the Ruby Mountains, snow-capped, blush gentian. *Goiko mendian elurra dago.* In the mountains there is snow/ down in town it is still August. *Go forth and set the world on fire! God created man to work.* Opus Dei.

You lost, cowboy? the woman's voice startled him to a military attention. Where had she come from? Was she his Marilyn?

Euzkaldune? Was it that obvious? Was he a cowboy then or was he a Basque? Could she tell? Dumbstruck by her height and by her ... he continued to observe the oddly disconcerting apparition as a sure sign of his redemption and deliverance, but, Grace Echevarria was as imposing and unexpected as the Ruby Mountains were tall (and nearly as tall). Arrived he had to Paradise, but clear skies notwithstanding, on the surface of things it was the *puta* dust he hadn't quite expected. *Autsa txoko guztietan.* Dust in every nook and cranny. Wasn't even brimstone solid rock until it burned?

What's your naame? Yeah, you there. (*Dios mío.* God, not yet.) For the life of him Joxe could not tell this tall apparition in blue *vaqueros* who he really was (Could he? *Quoi faire?*) This was his second major setback after having left from the airport in Bilbao, the first being the cruel necessity of next day departure from Manhattan to this wild western Paradise USA Nevada-style.

I'm Grace, said the blonde who to his great regret towered above him.

I am José. I am a a Jes-uit," he stammered.

Jesus, whas that? Sounds like a sneeze. Jeez, are you ok? (At least a trace of concern on the high cheek-boned face.)

Ok ok I am . . . Joe. Yes, that's it, he replied quite stupidly.

Ok then, Joe, I'm takin ya to Echevarria's. Tha be awright with you? (Everything was "ok" as long as she stayed there standing on the sidewalk with him.)

Wasting neither time nor words, the girl snatched the priest's suitcase motioning him over to a Ford flatbed its nether wheels parked halfway on the curb. Turn right then left: in four minutes flat he was right on Main Street downtown Paradise. (*Or would it be "uptown"?*)

There ya go, Joe, she said definitively pointing to a four-story brick building with a sign he finally recognized as "Echevarria," his carded destination.

Curiously enough, the Basque "hotel"-bar (now no restaurant) would be his home for the time being: there was no rectory in Paradise, no place for the priest but the inn. Still, he was puzzled. What did she mean? Was *he* the one to "go"? Now? Or was *she*? Then? Was her "there" in fact "here"? His place now this or *that*? Had he really looked like a cowboy or was she mocking him? At least she hadn't said, "Hello, sheepherder": That offered him some relief.

Why was he so stupid with women? Why did he always have to think about everything he thought? he thought. What he wanted was Manhattan! What he wanted was to be St. Ignatius de Loyola on his way to Paris. Lope de Aguirre seeking El Dorado at the very least. What he *really* wanted was to turn inside out on the hot sidewalk in front of his American Girl, eviscerate himself to demonstrate the tender inner rills of his burning soul—what stuff he was really made of. What he wanted was to throw open the flaps of his raincoat like a peddler on the Champs d'Élysées, show her his watches. What he wanted was to show her *all* his goods. Even over tall as she was, right then and there he would take her. The long legs, that blue highway of denim. The eyes. The long blond hair.

He sure was a short glass of water, she thought. No, a fish with *no* water to be outa. Better git him to gittin down the street. She pointed him on again to the four-story hotel, this time like an Aussie nudged him (just a little bit) into the front screen door which opened directly to the bar. The last thing she wanted was to talk to Amuma. Gregoria Echevarria was getting on in years and always carried a pistol. She was a crack shot, but recently suffered from cataracts *and* glaucoma: Today delivering the little package, Grace wasn't up to taking any chances.

Now over eighty, her grandmother had lost her right arm and breast, with all those lymph nodes to the cancer, but none of her *gatza*. She was still full of fire and brimstone and piss and vinegar. Still missing Aitxitxe grandfather as she said, *lika sonofabeech*. Refusing to enter the hotel herself, Grace looked her pilgrim up and down (which didn't take long) and turned on her heel on the curb in front of Echevarria's. Perhaps this Father Joe was not exactly what they were expecting. Could they send him back? Maybe they should.

There now. You'll be awright. They'll know what to do with ya in there, she said more kindly giving him a nudge with her voice like a sheepdog. Why was the idiot looking at her that way? For cryin out loud, what was he doing? He seemed half loco this leppie. Maybe start all over and gentle him in.

Ongi etorri. Welcome home.

(You must be the new priest, mister.)

1962

The church is cold as a witch's tit or a tomb. It is snowing, a cold Nevada Easter. *Esaten da*, they said there were still more than twenty Basque herders holed up at Echevarria's for winter which was one hell of a party. *Auxe fandango!* There'd be more to confess than Father Joe cared to think about: his business would be picking up soon. How does one sin in a sheep camp or on the four hundred mile range to Long Valley except by "intention" any way? The catechism of these Basque boys wasn't good enough for the kind of sophistication required by the Catholic church much less its New

Vatican II. (It was a waste of a rigorous Jesuit education!) Thanks to the Jansenists, they say Basques don't have sex any way they just sing about it half-drunk.

Nevertheless, when the herders made it to town the big dirty accounted for 90 percent of confessions if you could rope em in when they came to town (which wasn't easy). Father Joe wasn't even sure if they really comprehended the other five real biggie venals and their menials were so many they could never remember. This new ecclesiastical calculus would take some time to sort out in this arch diocese called Sweet Promised Land. The easy part, thought Father Joe, was that young, healthy men, given half a Chinaman's chance speak uniformly the same single sin. He might be Father Joe of Paradise—a priest, but he was still a man. He was no fool either: he had clear directions. *For when Moses was about to erect the tent. He was instructed by God saying, "See that you make everything according to the pattern that was shown you on the mountain."*

Elizatik urreanena

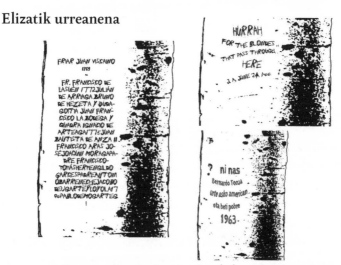

So many years in America / and always poor.

Grace

In the end, it was the sun-warmed scent of her skin that would be his undoing—all that golden hair.

Elko Daily Free Press, August 5, 1964

Highlighting the National Basque Festival Dance Saturday evening at the Elks Lodge on Idaho Street above Sewell's will be selection and naming of the Queen of the Festival. Mrs. Earl Shobe and and Mrs. La Mar Kendall, co-chairmen of the queen contest, said the names of the six girls will not be released until after the judging.

As he said Easter mass he felt a reassuring sweetness come all over him: God was real and the blessed Jesus. Hail. Mary Blessed Mother of Grace grace grace. Her name was Grace (what cruel cosmic joke?) and she was his All American Girl: a tall blonde with slant green eyes. Her limbs so long he felt like Vasco de Gama anticipating the Cape of Good Hope. Vasco de Gama with his six sons—*alcalde-mor* of Sines Castle.

So many girls! So much fresh American skin:
blondes, brunettes, redheads of a second, a third! gen-
eration of hybrid vigor. What beauty! What pain—
such tortures not even Dante could describe.

Let us proclaim the mystery of faith: *Aie Ama! Enee . . .*
Her lips, Lord. Her lips.
Kyrie eléison
Lord, have mercy
You wished me well
Christ! have mercy
You couldn't tell
That I'd been cryyyying
Christ has died.
Christ is risen.
Christ will come again.
The Body of Christ
The body of Christ
The . . . body . . . of
The mass is ended: Go in peace. Thanks be to God!

Tran, tran. . . The color of her tongue. Lord Jesus! He
asked the blessed Virgin for the blessing of her mouth
only taking Holy Communion. *Hostias.* He would be
her priest. Her Host.

> The Humboldt Star, November 27, 1912
>
> "Basque Priest will visit North-
> ern section" Father Enright of Love-
> lock, accompanied by Father Hippolite
> Topet of Los Angeles, left yesterday
> morning by automobile for Paradise.
> Father Topet is of Basque nationality
> and comes to do spiritual work for any
> of his countrymen.

What happen to man, Father?

That which happens to all men. Death.

I no wanna go to hell Thas where dey aways tell me go.

Confess and repent. What is your sin, my son?

Bizi naiz. I live.

Zein errua? What are your sins?

Eroa zuen very bad accidente. He no die right away, Joxe.

In nomine Patri et fillie . . . In the name of the father

Errua derrigorrezkoa da ala? Is it a bad one?

All sin is original. Is it Helen again?

Ellen Ellen I tell you Ellen. No goddamn Hell-en.

Have you . . . ?

Zer pentsa zu? Wha you thinkin a me? *María, Jesús y José!*

Is she a married woman?

Ezetz. No no.

Did you . . .

Yes, Fa-der, *bi aldiz.*

Two times? I must know details to determine your penance.

We go *kanpu santuan.* The cemeteries is quiet place no one bother you. My hands all softs from *la lanolina* from shearin. She say I do the, I her wild Basque warrior *Aia aiééiiiihii!*

Aurrera, go on, son.

Son? You three years older me Joxe! She tole me take her down dere and, like a sheeper with a sheephooker I take her fast like a lambs, like wolf of the forest Basajauna, thas me.

Did you, did you . . . finish, it then?"

Ziztua bizian. Zast! Just like that, *mutil.*

"Aita" or "Father" to you, please.

Aita-or-Father-To-You-Please, I do another one.
Beste bat!
Another one? You mean that quick?
You godamnbetchya.
(*Kristau*) Was this high desert Paradise heaven or
was it hell. In summer it sure felt like Dante's Inferno.
Zerua ta inpernua baita. Both. *Tximistua* like light-
enings on Rubies. Bringin fire, bringin rain, Joxe.
Is that the only one, this time?
No, but there is aways grace. Right, Father Joxe?
(Grace?)
Joxe, you think I take the citizen ship USA?
Father, please, *mecedes,* have mercy on me.
It is God's will. That all will come later.
Later, you help me get papers, Father Please?
You know the law. 90 days *provisional.*
Tha Julio at Spanish Rancho say third stay now
you go out, you come back in you go again. Sonetines
the owners hole out the monies til the end no interes,
cheap bastards *euzkaldunak* too! You marry American
girl you made it, *ezta?* Dere other ways too tha Julio
say. Lotsa herders *permanentes* now. They no difference
than me. In America it's the law. Ya gots to find the
loops holes. We all poor sonsabitch sheepers. You help
me, Joxe ok?
In the name of the father and the—
Hey, whazat ingelesa? Why in Inglesh, Joxe?
That's Vatican II.
Ze demonioa? What the hell you say. It still count
for me?
Aitaren. . . in the name of the Father and the son
and—
¡*En Latín, hijole!* You head got all missed up. What
you need, Joxe is a gulfren. I get you one, you get me

paperak legals.
    . . . *filis.* You owe me three Our Fathers, two Hail
Marys, four
    You confusin me. I do em all twice this time. Need
extras for next tine. You get me citizenship, I get you
girl, ok José?
    No Basques getting citizenship now. Your stay *es
provisional,* Dominic. You've stayed too long. Time's
up.
    Will you fix me all ups, Joxe?
    Bai zera, I'll fix you, Txo Txo. I will.

Elizatik urrunena

AMERIKANUAK, WILLIAM DOULGASS AND JON BILBAO

```
In 1959 the Immigration Service began to
grant extensions but these were limited in
June 1963 to two per herder for a maxi-
mum of ninety days each. In the mid-1960s
herders were allowed to return for a third
stay . . . In 1965 there were 1,283 herd-
ers in the American West under contract to
the Western Range Association and 97 who
had been imported under the Wyoming Wool-
growers Sheepherder Procurement Program.
```

Amorem tui solum cum gratia
    your love and your grace

1972
Echeberry
Lee

Ne mai' aikuu nanisuntahaih takwahkunt'l imassin,
        supai en nanittsawihkantu'I

I think he's sweet on ya, Ellie.

I'm gunna talk to the boys. You stay put now, ya hear?

Getting no response, the roper lassoed a snarl round his whiskey-soaked words.

You listen to me goddamit, Leonora. You got it, girl?

Stunned, the girl held still and did not answer. She never had a chance. Fast the cowboy grabbed her and like the bull dogger that he was twisted her to him till she heeded his word.

Ok. I'll stay put.

It was the time of night things had yet to be decided, the dust neither kicked up nor settled. No one was drunk enough yet at the Paradise Sheepherder's Ball: the battles for territory and females had not yet begun, horns had not yet locked. There was good tension in the air: no one drunk enough yet to care about fighting. Cowboys and Indians, Bascos from Paradise, Winnemucca and Jack Creek, some high school kids hoping to score a beer and a girl still stood erect, spit and polish: all dandied up and relatively serene. The night was young: the loose ice cubes in the galvanized horse trough still surrounded the bottles of Miller, cans of Coors, Seven-Up and Diet Pepsi. It was a good time. The ice, still hard and cold around the cold keg of Bud.

Wanna dance, Elle? Bernardo Urrizaga asked her.

I cain't, she said.

Tha your boyfriend over there? The one eyein us there?

I guess.

Come on, it's a jota less go. *Goizen neska*, the Basque boy said wearily, his bota bag near empty.

Better stay here. *Eskerrik asko* though.

Your loss then . . . *Aupa!* He laughed as he turned from her moving on to the next possible conquest. Maybe he'd get her on the chicken dance or a waltz.

The bodies shifted again after Jota Navarra #2 and the porrusalda ended. A Charley Pride tune sweetly droned on as the dancers looked to change partners or not.

> *The secret I'm speaking of*
> *is a woman and a man in love*
> *and the answer is in this song*
> *that I always sing. . .*

The derelict and the desperate stared down at the tips of their boots, drew imagined figure eights in the sawdust: corral posts, lazy Zs there on the dance floor as young girls huddled like sheep for cover in a giggling solidarity of grace. Elle moved her way furtive towards a gal band, saw Linda Duferrena from out the PX. She and Linda had done "Make it With Wool" together in 4-H. Linda always won.

Heh, girl. Arenchya with Jess Lopategui?

Not no more.

Who'd ya come with then?

Rocky Roa.

No way.

Way.

He's just after a piece a ass, Ellie. Whatchya doin with that bronc rider then? He ain got no ranch.

No, but I do.

Hank Williams was heatin things up awright. The cold armory light hardened the faces of the goin-to-get-drunks. Twelve thirty, the fun not yet over, but the evening was on the edge of a wane. The buckaroos fidgeted in their tight Wranglers as middle-aged sheep men and ranchers, all thinning hair and paunches, dragged their wives or hopefuls out on to the dance floor for polkas, waltzes and two-steps. Something was stirring by midnight filling the armory with some feeling oddly bent on hope, but promising sure disaster. The cattlemen moved on to Eddie Arnold and Chet Atkins, making one last do-see-do of it before Jimmy Jausoro took over in his famed accordion madness about 1:00 a.m. At the Paradise Sheepherder's Ball the Anglo tunes were preliminaries only—for stiffer hips and withered loins—before the real fun begins. One last time around, aging domesticated hombres sniffed yanking trousers up over their paunches; as their women, Gramma, Mom and Aunt Sally, raised fleshier arms to fasten their hair in one last bobby-pinned hope. As the accordion began the Basque thing again, something rope-taut and twisted stirred up like a dust devil out on a board-walked street.

The Shoshoni stood there, still expectant. His brothers watching him out the corners of their eyes.

Who you think *you* are? Tonto? Whachaya lookin at anyways?

That, there, Rocko, is Echeberry Lee, the sidekick chimed in wedging a wad of Copenhagen in the slime pocket of his lower lip.

The fuck you say. What kinda name is that for an Injun?

Donchya know his story, boy? It's a good un.

> *Something I will always remember were the natives of Saipan, the Chamorros. They looked a lot like us (Indians). During the battle, at night, they would approach us, trying to surrender. We couldn't trust the Japs, so we couldn't take any chances and we had to shoot. All along the front lines were old men, children lying dead each morning. During the battle at Saipan, we found a little boy, about the age of three. He was crying and I lifted him from the arms of his dead mother and he just clung to me. I think maybe he did this because of my dark skin. We were on the front lines still moving. I kept him with me for about an hour or so until the First Aid people came along. Then I turned him over to them and we went on. I often wonder what became of him. Arthur Timothy Manning U.S. Marine Corps Sergeant*

En nean appettsi nemmi manemenaippehkanten

Why, this here Echeberry Lee they found him half-starved out on the desert by Currie, out to Twelve Mile Creek. His grandma had up n died on him and that was all there was left of his people and the others wouldn't take him cause they said he had the ghosts *Tso'appeh* on his back *bitsuseN*. They was all spooked a his blue eyes: *Taipo, taipo! Dibo, dibo!* they shouted. Not *Newe*, not Injun, not the people, not us. *Wosa, wosa* born of woe, the one with a burden basket: Boy *Wosa*.

The Echeberrys took him in for a while, but he was wild as a goddamned Banshee, like a bronc that jes wouldn't be broke, so ole Hank Echeberry and his boys get in the pickup and drive down to Carson City took him out to that Stewart Indian School they did. He cain even read and won speak and the teachers think he's retarded, ya know? He's jus a little dude, only speaks Shoshone. He'd been with his grandma so long outta school and all before they found him out dryin up on the desert out there.

Taipo, Taipo, white man, outsider, enemy, was all he said and them not listening.

Takkumpahkwa, Takkunmpahkwa, killed by hitting rock, he tries no way to explain.

They couldn make no sense of him atall. *Tontsia, toonampih,* flower chokecherry *toyama tua* brave son of the mountain. It was all jus bullshit. So the teachers ask the other Shoshoni kids how to say food *tekkappehp'ai*. They keep him starvin for days, there like a dog, try to bribe him. It don work. Then they whip him in the back *kwahai* within an inch of his life and chain him to a chair in the basement *tuttsappeh tuu tutuanneen* with other dark children in the dungeon there in the underground. His fingernails scraping *masitoonmo'oma*, he gets the hand bindings loose, tries to scratch out his own eyes *mo'oma* with one hand. In a little while *kaap-pai* he finally speaks. He tells them.

Appema'ai had a father *haim'ai* with an uncle. *Usen matianten, mai, uten ipaka weneten.* He fierce one, they say, one standing this tall. *Kunai taka yaakkan-tem miauy.* He carry firewood in summer on his back. *Usewaihten, mai.* He is like that, they say. *Toyapittan Nananewe, mai usen tanniikwina.* He is called Man of the Mountain, he tries to tell them. They do not listen. They cannot hear him.

What is yur name, boy?

Toyapittan Nannewe.

Your Christian name?

Toyahpittan Nannewe, mai usen tannikwina. He is called Son of the Mountain. *Usewaihten, mai,* the old people say.

Yur last name? Family name?

Toyapittan Nan. The beatings begin again, a cross is laid on his chest in the dungeon; he knows the black-robed exorcists will come again to get him. Why can't he die? *Hai, Hai en nean appettsi nemmi manmenaippehkante.* He looks like he has grease *yuhu yuhu* all over him excrement and urine. *Tsa'I ait-en nanah tawittiakap-pehni napuni, un kwitapphe, un siipeh.* He goes down to the old place to hide away from the voices, away from the words. *New to'opekkaku, newi tsayetseppehkanten, mai tenniikwippeh.* When a person gets sick, he raised them up. *Akkhuh himpai mmannaisen en newi statyetse'iten* from the earliest time. You have raised up the healed people *Dani'bine Hai.* You You are born again *Hai Hai* Lord Jesus.

En aisen sokoppehpa'an nemmi tekippeh-kanten

```
Elko Daily Free Press, May 12, 1939
Final payment by the United States
Government was made today for the
Ogilvie ranch at Lee. The 1,500 acre
Ranch on the South Fork was purchased
as part of the federal project for set-
tling the Indians. Sale price of the
ranch was $50,000. Mr. and Mrs. P.J.
Ogilvie moved to Elko some time ago
from Lee. Their son, George, has re-
mained on the the ranch, but will give
up possession soon, at which time he
and his family will move to Elko where
he will establish himself in the in-
surance business.
```

Your namenamenamename? Beaten, the boy
answers . . .

Echeberry Lee.

Stupid boy. Echeberry is the name of the people
who found you. That's your last name. Lee is where you
came from, the reservation. Is it a Basco name? Tonto.
What the hell then, you'll be Lee Echeberry.

Echeberry, Echeberry, Lee.

Echeberry ni ne Echeberry nenene ni ni naz Lee me.

And that's what everybody called him then,
Echeberry Lee. It's stupid an ass backwards, but it kinda fits him.

How the hell did he git back to Paradise?"

I guess he bit some minister guy who was tryin to
do 'im, and they called the Echeberrys out to Lee and
told em they could come get him else he'd go to the
state mental institution.

And they went an got him?

Go figure. They got Bob Goicoechea to do it. Boy
don talk. Echeberry boys, Bernardo an Pedro, take

freak round like a guide dog or somethin. He goes to
the fair dances too, like a dancin bear, ya know? Don
mess with him though or those Basco boys'll kick your
ass. They call him "brother" —such phony ass bullshit.
    He's a dummy?
    Pretty much.
    Whaz he doin talkin to my girl then?
    Jes cause he cain talk don mean his nuts don work.
    You fuckin cunt. You mind me. Ya hear now? Ya
hear?
    Mmhuh.
    Whazat now, girl?
    I hear ya.
    I'm the man here. The Man. You do what I say. *You
belong to meeee* . . . The song soaking into her like oil on
a dry rope tightening her brain then ringing her neck.
    It grew late; his friends would be watching for her.
The wood plank over the beer trough slipped loose
shifted side long away by a hurtling body and the beer
trough holding melted water was no more. Cans were
scattered and some of them had exploded, and that,
son, was a serious matter. It was only a matter of time
for the big fight to begin, either in the middle of the
floor or out by the double doors.
    *The only gold I have for you is in this wedding band/
Cause all I have to offer you is meee* . . .
    Even though she'd been just a little girl when it
happened to that Messican, Elle could still smell the
piss rot fear like mold damp hay of him. Later, his
fresh dead scent: the urine of the paddocks, the rank of
the last mud creek gone fetid from the slew of his life.
Known for bein ornery, he'd finally bit it at a fair dance
upstairs above Sewell's Market at the BPOE. Sometimes at night she'd still see his crazy skull cracked

upon like a watermelon him fightin some Paiutes. He lay there dragged behind the velvet curtain of a stage prop, spread-eagle laid out like Christ almighty: a a living memory no one would ever forget. The gash up his lip marked the swelling of a broken nose in a long living signature of blood. They'd pummeled him good, looked like the dead loser KO'ed in a prize fight she'd seen at Grammar #1 once with her uncle Pedro. Someone observant at the dance had noticed he'd stopped breathing though and that was the real trouble. Even that hadn't stopped the cowboy dance that came just once a year. It was Charley Pride again. Now everbody knew old Charley was a nigger, but that didn matter much with eight tracks in a pick-up right up until MTV.

Mama said later telling it all again to a neighbor woman out to the PX: *Tha Alice Goicoechea, head of the Home Arts on the fair board finished it and finally done her Christian civic duty and called the police. Without no stretcher in the dance hall two flights up above Sewell's Market at the BPOE and thinking all hope was lost on him anyway two buckaroos out from Jimmy Stewart's Wine-cup (or was it Bing Crosby's?) dragged tha Messican feet first out the side door wrapped up in the stage curtain so no one would notice him.*

Vividly still, she remembered his coarse black hair, this Mexican: a bristly paintbrush all spread out an odd whoosh of blood arced across as he fell reminding her of a downed bull she'd once seen with her Aitita in the old Garcia rodeo ground days. The same red swath crimsoned maroon by the dust unaltered bright, the same deep slow death. *Una muerte sin honra.* No honor. Just death.

> **The Free Press, March 1, 1922.**
>
> Maggie Dixon, an Indian squaw, was found on the streets in an intoxicated condition last evening and was taken by two obliging strangers to the court house where she spent the night. It was discovered this morning that this, her first offense, was occasioned by the death of a near relative.

Boys, where's my bitch?

Elle went outside as she was told to do. Broke loose for a minute—she wanted to run. Incongruously, a Lynn Anderson song was playing after Boga, Boga Jimmy Jausoro. So buxom sweet the peroxide blond "I Never Promised You a Rose Garden." As the Basque conjunto took a break and the disc jocky changed tracks, some dancers spilled out for a smoke leaving others to linger on till one thirty, maybe two. He'd be spittin mad at her, he would. If drunk enough, he might just smack her again. Panicked, Elle looked at the dark parking lot for the stock truck Chevy. Either he'd moved it or she hadn't been paying attention. The moon so bright just this side of the sun "The Girls All Git Prettier At Quittin' Time," it was now about 1:00 a.m.

The fairground lot next to the armory was oddly luminous as if all the smoke from the bar had cleared. *Les jus' step out here for a breath of fresh air, gal.* The parking lot was bathed in a high blue cool; she felt birthed right here in the dirt lot outside. Loosed from the girlish flock a gals she felt vulnerable again like she'd cut free from the herd only again to be wrangled. Made her think oddly of the Ducks Unlimited banquet she'd attended with a beau from FFA as a freshman: their proud banquet proclamation patriotically preserving wetlands saving wildlife for spring wetlands, raising money for fall flyways so we brave hunters can zap them for a more exotic Thanksgiving. We, brothers in arms, shall healthfully free these beautiful creatures, allow them to grow to full adulthood to migrate to be shot down in one clean green mallard careening from the sky. At the banquet, like a big shot, that same boyfriend had bought silver-engraved duck lithographs copied from US postal service stamps licensed to the intermountain states: Montana, Wyoming, Idaho, Utah, Colorado, Nevada and given them to her Aita for Christmas. Dad had thought she should marry him right then and there.

Nowhere to hide out, nowhere to go. It had all been decided long before—her life, her fate set in country concrete only her future was only creosote dirt. *Aita* would only pay for year only at The U *zelako bullshit ori Leonora!* Then she'd have to come home to Madariaga & Echevarria Inc. No one needed a cowboy poet out here, least of all a girl. What a cattle ranch needed was a brood mare that doctored, ran errands and cooked (especially that cooked). He'd be her lovey dovey cowboy boy for a year or two having landed a ranch. Then she'd get some youngins. They'd fatten some calves in 4H for the kids to show at the fair, butcher in fall, fill the freezer. She'd gather elderberries and choke cherries in Lamoille Canyon in September, put em up as syrup and jelly by Halloween. They'd come into town monthly, shop at Farmer's Supply, eat a French Dip at The Stockmen's. And as she tended at night to the babies in the hotel room, he'd be down bullshitin horsetradin—chasin pussy at the bar. They'd all pretend a viable *Western Stockman* kinda life until her Daddy saw too many bruises on her shoulders and show the rodeo cowboy (for a while) the door.

She knew they'd shop at JC Penney's, get supplies at PM Supply owned by a third cousin, go to Skagg's for prescriptions, Western Auto for tires: one day even pizza and McDonald's would come to town and son that was progress. She already knew the clothes they'd wear from Capriola's, the diesel sound of the 350 flat-bed Ford; the feed bills and taxes that gathered disorganized on the kitchen counter, the fights, the yelling, the mud and doctor's bills. She knew she'd outgrow the tight-pegged Wrangler's after youngins. The hips'd start to spread hips gradual-like: like a heifer gone all to perpetual milk. She'd get too sunburned in the hay fields lending a hand. Her hands would grow callused and the heels of her feet would crack something painful swell with each pregnancy. Despite the high myth, the hot-sunned weariness of ranch life and its dead frozen cold would settle in celluloid fat pockets on her buttocks, carve out deep crevasses, finally to draw fine little fissures across her mouth time carving one slit vicious arroyo up between her eyes. Six kids'd pull on her tits, all born before she was thirty-two.

Then one fine day hot in summer she'd take the 150 alone into town, buy a cherry slush at the Dairy Queen, and drive to the Paradise Clinic. There, she'd beg threaten and cajole ole Doc Moren into a fast D & C. There was only one way to pay for a ranch and keep a horse trailer loaded, to the Paradise County Fair goin' and that was to put up or shut up—no longer be Elle, no longer be she. It would then be too late.

Lost your way, little lamb? Why don you dance with meee? I'm waitin for my boyfriend."

Where's his truck then?

Over there. I'll be goin.

Ya think so? Do ya?

She knew the tone, the drill so well slip slidin away it as like the veil was gone off a the livin an he Daddy Santa Claus Mayor of the Knights of Columbus had ripped off the slick costume from the five n dime on Main Street.

You got purdy hair . . . She thinks her shit don' stink. Whad she say there any ways, Tommy?

Her only hope was the whiskey, hope it had left him limp-legged and bareback. Maybe she could run across the field past the high school into the cemetery where at least it was dark. At the very least she could hide among the dead and the sleeping: At twenty-two she'd already had enough of life anyway. She walked through the greened aisles dotted by headstones. In the moonlight she read the names like the familiar obituaries of her life. They were all there planted like bulbs, her people, her clan. All there still, her familiars—her family lying stoned in the moonlight. Her people. Aitxitxe Grandfather.

MADARIAGA

JOSE
1896–1972

JOE MENDI
1877–1948

YGNACIO
1910–1932

PAS
MENDY
AND
BABY

So much time had passed, the tombs of names weighted her down—she was exhausted, needed only to sleep. As she walked the stones, she listened for them. The moon lit her pathway, a soft wind billowing. Her head was lull-filled with moonlight and singing. Aittita alive again. She was a little girl on the ranch dreaming of the day. Amuma was singing. They had eaten *barakatsalda, tortilla de patatas, café con leche* garlic soup potato omelet and buckaroo coffee oversweetened with condensed milk before bedtime. They were happy. It was time to sleep. *Ofera jun!* Off to bed, you! Time to sleep, sleep. Basque lullaby . . .

> Folding buds as they pass by
> lullaby, whisper and sigh,
> Lullaby, lullaby.
> Lullaby, Twilight is spreading
> silver wings over the sky

En nanisuntahaihten
It made her not shamed, but shy to be so close to them. It felt awkward always being among the dead, so delicious yet frightful in the first world awash silvery across time. Each time she wanted to stay with them forever, but they kept pushing her back. *Danak Jainkoak eiñak gire/zuek eta bai gu ere.* We all are God's creation/You and us too. Be alive now *bizi-bizije oraintxe.* Don't sleep, no sleep.

The Shoshoni stood there. His brothers watching him wary out the corners of their eyes.

Jesus! You scared me. You Echeberry Lee?

Cain you speak to me then? She went on stupidly feeling the idiot, went on hoping that more words, more syllables would coax him from his silence.

You hear me now, do ya? Cain you hear me now, you Echeberry Lee? Was he stupid or a dummy? Maybe it was because he was real Injun with no family or schooling. Who knew about Injuns?

We better sit down. Awright now, Echeberry Lee?

Aie Ama! Oh my, she gasped looking at him under her breath barely audible. The damn fool was eating some god awful plant that looked like a lupine he'd pulled up in the field on his way to the rock yard. He offered her a stem with the most perfect leaf attached.

No, thank you. I've eaten. The boy dogged her like a calf. No shakin him either.

Echeberry Lee? You wanna walk with me? Awrighty then. Les go. And he went.

She thought he had understood? His lean shape, new Wranglered and booted, topped by a Levi jacket lined in red flannel was graceful and fluid. The muscles in long lines bunched and released the spare young maleness of him. As she watched him rise, he turned and smiled and they walked through the grave markers tomb-stoned deafened to life.

Oh, you, we better get ya home now, ya hear?

His dark eyes glistened blue wet in the moonlight. Tender, tender is this night of our beginning: the oldest story ever told. Her mind raced wildly let loose like a filly in alfalfa. It couldn't be happening! He was the smell of fresh mown hay, late dew dark still in dawn. Gallant and shy, he offered his arm to her in the gesture of the expectant groom all tall Gary Cooper. She said they would walk, but this felt like dancing, rhythmic wonderful dancin in three quarter time. This their eternity. Now their time.

Ohikua nauzu I have chosen you to love / *ez nauzu kanbiatu* I am the same, I have not changed / *bihotzian beinin hartu* my heart has chosen youououo

In the moonlight they were bathed. In the moonlight they were christened. When together they stopped near a water spigot she caught, sidelong-shy, her first real glance of him: the face etched painful, a cenotaph revealing a tell-tale heart.

She watched him now covertly careful: his nostrils' sudden flare, heard the low breath softly soughing, the rawhide skin of him glistening hairless, the skin of him where the cloth hadn't covered it all Cordova leather. The inside of his neck below each ear running into his collared chest was caramel, chamois where she nestled where he murmured. Next him now as her heart beat madly, Elle near Lee near fainted fast from desire. *Maitea, non zira?* / *W*here are you, my love? She could barely breathe as he sang to her the old songs again. *Upitaan á* slow down so she would understand *Upitaÿ* so that this time would last.

Lullaby.

> *Haurtxo txikia seaskan dago*
> The babe is in the cradle
> *Zait irudi aingerua lo*
> looking like an angel asleep
> *Ene maitea, ene potxolo*
> my dear love, little baby
> *Egin ezazu lo ta lo*
> sleep now, sleep
> Pointing touching with fingers touching . . .
>
> *Bambi* head burua

He left her suspended in honey to bees susurrezzz, suspended there cradled in their twilight daze. *Loa loa lo kutun berde.* Gently. The sprinklers came on at the top of the low hill casting a soft burry mist over plush green ground. *Tsaanten naipin* pretty girl *Tsaanten, naipen naipen.* Half dozing remembered now the past which had become them. Grandfather *kenuma'ai* grandfather *ne tsoo* great grandfather time *natemakahtaippeh* sold off *natonnuyuahtaipeh* pushed *awa nawoi Newe* with the child grandmother is listening *utsi ne kahni* my house *utzi* leave my house *kohnon* with a cradle board *pa'a* high up *hipikkwa* ran quickly *hupa* first good. He had a lifetime to tell her. Could she listen?

Goobai forehead *bekokia*

Mai it is said. *Mai Mukua* her spirit *mi'ahtaippeh* left a long time ago *Naappeh* used to be *naappehkanten* used to be like that *Natonnuyvahtaippeh taippeh!* was pushed away *Dibo Dibo ne ne Taibo ne natonnuyvahtaippeh* water still babies left alive on the river's edge *pa'ohaa* their stillborn haunting the People thought *gai gai gai Newe* he he *u u* had bad spirit within no not not *gai* the People *Dibo Taibo gai gai* white white *ne Newe ni naz ni* I am white not you I *ne Newe* you.

Do'yoM neck *lepoa*
tympai lips *ezpainak*

There was no one else in the world to hold her now. No one else to listen. He had captured her quickly because he had never tried. That was his secret: this she knew. Forgetting them both now she knew only how time stood still.

Newe Hai Newe The People Shoshoni *neweneen nittoihpenni* singing grandmother soup *en hupa* your soup *Haintsehpa'I* I have a *friend api* over here *awelia*in with a cup. *A'anna* somewhere children *emma'ari ekko'ihka* sleep with you sleep with you two. *Tsaanten naipen* pretty girl pretty girl *ekko'ihka* sleep sleeps. *Hittoon hup loa loa lo kuttun berde. Txakur andia etorriko da/a* big, bad dog will come for you *zuk ez-baduzu egiten lo* / If you don't sleep sleep . . .

When the dew had begun to settle and the hair on her forehead to damply curl, *bambi ga'I bambi* he slowly unfolded his legs where she rested long along his thighs. He resettled the girl then in his arms and listened to her, watching. At the break of day when her brown eyes opened unto his blue ones, and he saw that now she was unafraid, he said the last words he would ever say and she answered with her heart. *Dehimbe biotza.* Thou art. *Dana'bine* eternaled. All their worlds hurtled together under the greened moonlight in one long while. Their words no longer mattered. The stones told their names.

ECHEBERRY LEE

ELEONORA

1982
Anastacia
Echeverria

There is a remarkable story current among the Chinese with regard to Li Hung Chang's ancestry. According to this legend it was during the days of sailing communication between America and the Celestial Kingdom that a Chinaman landed in Western America. He was known as Ah Li and claimed lineal descent from a celebrated Chinese writer who flourished about 1,000 years before Christ named Li Ling. Ah Li got among an unknown tribe of Indians in the West. He became a member of the tribe and was identified with them for years, taking part in many of their hunting expedition. In fact, Ah Li so distinguished himself in the chase that the tribe raised no objections when he offered to wed a maiden of the tribe. The young people were united and, following the tribal custom, lived in a separate wigwam. There was an absence of feasting, the European idea of wedding feasts was as yet unknown to the Indians. In a subsequent hunting expedition Ah Li was one of the party. During his absence the expected happened—it was a boy. A great feast was prepared for the father's return. It must be understood that Ah Li spoke the language of his wife's people. At the great feast he told the people about the great country across the salt waters, which he would like his wife and child to see. The little boy grew to be a favorite in the camp to the day his parents left the tribe for China. The wife died in China, the son visited his Indian relations once. He became a very wealthy man and took a leading part in Chinese public affairs. The Chinese contention is that this half-breed is Li Hung Chang's grandfather. There are many plausible incidents in support of this curious family history. In Chinese literature the matter is said to be historical, says a Mohawk Indian in the London Chronicle. The Free Press, December 12, 1901

June 1982, *Day 1*

ARTIFACTS. The archeological excavation, supervised by University of Nevada, Reno graduate students working under Prof. Donald Hardesty during 1999 to 2001, yielded many items. There were shards of pottery, bottles, jars, a rusted Log Cabin maple syrup tine, gaming pieces, Chinese medicine bottles, buttons, nails, a coffee machine, an abacus and fragments of pages of a Chinese book that discussed the new 1912 Republican government in China. The book and abacus probably belonged to the merchant China Lem. Found all over the 14 structures were Chinese stomach medicine bottles, indicating a common health problem. *The Chinese in Nevada,* Sue Fawn Chung.

I've hit something with my trowel.

Take the brush and start sweeping the dirt away gently.

It's flat on top like a chest or something.

Keep working it, slowly. No, with the artist's brush.

Man, this is not what I expected. They never tell you about the bugs, the sun, the dust.

You keep with it that's all.

For the big pay off at the end, the great discovery?

For when you want to start searching for something else.

Yeah, like a beer can. That's what I found yesterday. It was an old beer can. Ever seen one without a flip top?

Fascinating.

Not as glamorous as you thought?

It's just so long between epiphanies, I guess. You're out here cooking your brains out bent over like some coolie brushing dust off a piece of junk with a paintbrush—

Now you're getting it. Keep working.

I mean Jeezus, you diagram the position of a beer can like it was the emperor's diadem.

Is it any less important?

You know what I mean. It's just not . . .

Like in the movies?

Yeah, I mean are all artifacts created equal? Like

you take all this old stuff excavate, process, catalogue, categorize and study it years and years and try to put it all together on this totally infinitesimal level and maybe it isn't anything after all, ya know?

Then maybe it is.

How do you know what's important, Doc?

You don't. You hope and you keep working at it. Be careful when you remove that. The bottom is often not solid and will give way. You need to work around it.

Can I get it out now?

Have you plotted it *en situ* precisely?

What a drag. Why can't we just look at it?

It's part of the process.

Sounds like Tao Confucius says stuff. I say we rip out the treasure chest and sell the doubloons on the black market.

Unlikely anybody out here had much of a treasure.

He would beat her if she didn't find money this time. Gambling, he would ruin them, but he could not cook now standing with the mangled leg. The doctor said infection would kill him, anyway. Whose woman was she without him? Liberated or doomed?

This one, another millstone round her neck. Woman was born to suffering her grandmother had always said. At night in the dark before him— hahk sum—his black heart she wished him dead. A woman alone—the danger. As long as he lived (scoundrel and wastrel) her body was her own. He, her only slave master, she bowed as he had bowed all day. She slid the board back in the darkness reaching inside until her fingers grasped caressing silken hopeful the small pouch enclosed within the

chest. She breathed deeply dreaming of this girl
child grown strong, grown tall gone to her father's
house.

Why do you do this? It's so painstaking, so *unclear.*
I guess so.
At least you're tenured, published.
It changes nothing.
It doesn't? I thought that was the point.
So did I when I was your age.
Hey, look! It's a chest. Chinese characters. Maybe
there's buried treasure after all!
Now you can start on that northeast quadrant.
You're kidding. You want me to leave the buried
treasure and start on that manure pile over there?
It's a stable. This is a shack, probably a crib.
You mean they lived in a stable?
Not exactly. Crib as in whorehouse, a rookery with
chicks.
Look, this ground is charred. There must have been
a fire.

Born to pain, her little girl, Ana-sta-ci-a. Her back
ached with a vengeance tonight and the youngest
at four still suckled at her breast, dried her shriv-
eled, robbed her of needed strength. The two older
boys, put out to work at the mine contracted to the
whoremaster Old Lung. Hahk sum! Shanghai blood
sucker who drank his own people dry. The boys in
the trenches, underground. The young girls, bones
unformed, bodies bent permanently to the yoke of
the water bucket, to scullery work and laundry,
to the tending of animals. Gam daaih jek gap lá
chèvih gaai tiu. This Silver Mountain big frog

*hopping down the street, too big to be true. How was
this American hell different than the Chinese one?*

The Free Press, July 7, 1900

One of the "girls" of Chinatown took a
dose of poison Monday night, but Dr.
Hood managed to save her life with the
aid of a stomach pump.

The Free Press, December, 1887

At 6 o'clock last evening a blaze
started in a Chinese rookery on Front
Street, but fortunately was discovered and extinguished before it had
gained headway.

It's important to situate the artifact in its proper
context. You must envision the general, know the big
picture, before you can comprehend the specific.

Maybe it's full of gold coins and we can retire for
life.

Be careful what you ask for. The gods may grant
your wish.

Old Chinese saying?

Cinderella.

I thought you were, you know, Chinese.

I am American. My great great grandparents came
from Guangdong province Zhongshan after the Gold
Rush to Nevada as merchants. You know the rest of the
story. In Austin alone there was a Chinese population
of over a thousand. Tuscarora was said to be the largest Chinese settlement outside of San Francisco. At one
time as many as 2,000.

HONG LEE,
General Merchandise

Fine Display Rich Silks
Just Received, a Large Stock of
Chinese Rice Whisky
CALL AND BE CONVINCED
Everybody knows me as "Lem," and I have been in
business 18 years.
NO. 1 PEKIN AVENUE (CHINATOWN) GOLD
CREEK, NEVADA,

So where are they now, your people?
Underground. Their names here interred.
You're history!

> *Zai zi.* There were few women in the early days.
> Men to women, more than ten to one. In 1880 in
> Nevada there were 5,102 males to 314 females on
> *Yinshan* Silver Mountain. The American West
> was much more inter-racial than imagined.
> Bertha Coffee, whose mother was Native Amer-
> ican, lived with her Chinese father in Tonopah
> for many years. Still, intermarriage wasn't legal
> between Chinese and whites until just recent-
> ly. It wasn't until 1943 when the Chinese exclu-
> sion acts were repealed. Before that, interracial
> couples were subject to arrest. After that, just
> ridicule.

No way.
Way.
The 1875 Page Law strongly discouraged Chinese
women from emigrating. They had to officially prove
that they were not prostitutes which is hard to do if
you aren't one initially. It was a single-male worker so-
ciety, but about a third of Chinese here were married
with their wives living in China many of whom they

never saw again. Interracial couples were subject to arrest up until the 1950s.

You're shittin me.

I shit you not, Grasshopper.

The Free Press, May 25. 1889

The white woman who lived with a Chinaman in Carlin about a year ago, and whose daughter was found in Chinatown here, and arrested by Constable McAdams, has turned up in San Francisco. The Bulletin says: A lady engaged in missionary work in Chinatown, reported that a white woman with her small child was living in a cooped up room with with a Chinaman at 1008 Dupont Street, in a building entirely inhabited by Chinese. Officer Holbrook went to the place and found things were about as they had been reported. The woman said her name is Mrs. Clara Vail, or rather that was her name before she married the Chinaman, with whom she is at present living. His name is Yung Pang, and he claims to have been married to the woman in Suisun, Idaho, in June 1885 by a Judge Murray, but had lost the marriage certificate. They have been here two months, having come from Idaho. Mrs. Hung Pang is a native of New York, aged about forty. She says she has been married to two white men and treated badly by both. Her Chinese spouse has always treated her well, and she preferred Chinese to Whites. In the same room, which is only 8 x 12, and was in a filthy condition lived the little daughter of the woman, named Cora,

who was born April 16th, 1882, in Idaho. She is very pretty, but when found
by the officer was covered with dirt.
The mother stated that the whole family occupied one bed. She made some
objections to giving up her child,
but the officer told her that the girl
could not be permitted to remain there
among such surroundings and associ-
ates. She consented to let her go, and
Cora is now being taken care of by Miss
Bertha Powell 1416 Sacramento Street.
Mrs. Vail had another daughter, Rosa,
who is a little over sixteen years of
age, and quite good looking. She came
with her mother from Idaho. Upon her
arrival a young Chinaman named Ah Jim
commenced to pay a great deal of attention to her, and she came to regard him
with considerable attention. Ah Jim
wanted to marry her, and the girl consented, as did the mother. The two have
been living together for some time in
a lodging house on Dupont St., between
Sacramento and California, but have
not yet been married. When Officer
Holbook interviewed the Chinaman,
the latter Stated, "By and by I marry
her. She likes me and I like her." He
said that she had gone out that morning, but refused to say where. He was
told that he had better produce her or
there would be trouble for him. It is
rumored that the Chinese will sue out
writs of habeas corpus, and endeavor
to regain possession of the children.

I just thought of something. *You're* their artifact,
Suzy Wong. You're what's left of them! Can I excavate
you?

Impertinent grad student *kuli*. Don't you know your place?

Did you say "know your race"?

> *China Mary had a little coal left for a fire. She gathered her precious stash of twigs, dried rabbit brush, the split board from the mill ruin. Then set it all together and drew out a single long phosphorous match from the box hidden on the board which served as a shelf for what little they had. She blew carefully into the tinder, then cupped her hands about the warmth as she'd seen her mother do when she was a girl, long before she had been purchased, sent for to this new desert hell. Mary prayed the baby would not cry tonight, that he would be far enough gone to not want her just tonight. Tomorrow, The Other One would come. One silver dollar each time, each time for her cache. But they must be careful.*

There. It's all cleaned off. Now we can open it. Can't we?

It must first be plotted on the new schema.

I don't see why we have to invest all this time on details.

For the future. We must be careful—for them.

You got any kids?

My daughter is a civil engineer in Las Vegas.

Impressive. You made it.

Zim zim, little by little.

Pixkanaka-kanaka in Basque.

Sounds Japanese.

It must have been a lot harder for you than for your daughter.

I survived. American success story. Sweet Promised Land.

How about, you know, your people?

They lived. They did what they had to do. *Moun baan faat.* To each his own.

Or konpon. My Aitxitxe always says it. It literally means "Fix it on your own" "Get over it!" "Leave em alone." Kind of a Basque national anthem.

I thought you didn't have a nation. A very Confucian concept. You must have gotten it from us. *Móuh hàaih wàan kenk já.*

Which is?

"If there are no shoes grab the clogs and run."

Hey, the first Basque-Chinese phrase dictionary!

Chinese-Basque. We were first ya know.

The Basques are the Indians of Europe, proto-ante-European.

There was no Europe before China, no Europeans before Chinese civilization. *Bah lee bah leha.* Translation: This boy is good-looking?

Blah blah blah. This boy talks a lot.

Hey look, a button! It's perfectly preserved, cylindrical.

Should I plot it?

Yes, but leave it in situ. It's the only way to extract its story, with care and precision.

She prayed the extra nursing would save the baby. The song silent secret within her. The girl chatted petulantly, almost coquettish her attempt at speech. As her mother told her the old stories, the toddler, old at three to breastfeed, giggled happily parroting the singer, laughed at a fat snake-tailed rat scurrying from beneath the crib. Safe on her mother's lap now, the baby began to idly toy twirl-ing a long, loose button the blue coolie shirt worn threadbare.

So how did you go to Cal? Get a PhD and every-thing?

My parents had no son, no hope. My father's moth-er was half-white *hunzue* half-blood, "Jinx" they called her. They came to Nevada, Yinshan Silver Mountain with nothing from Gold Mountain, California with their parents who were merchants. They owned the New House Café, Carson City, Nevada, kind of a hum-ble boardinghouse for Chinese workers and other riff raff.

You were their Gold Mountain, Doc. You were their gold.

She waited listening reverent, patient, for the joy-ous crackling and took her babe the over-grown Ana to her breast as much for her own comfort as for the child's. The oval face, all black-eyed anx-ious, peered up at her mother filling her heart like a cup. She cherished this girl child all the more because he hated her, because she was female: defective, hard to put out to work. Through her daughter's clear steady gaze, the mother saw into the future. A-na-sta-cia. Ana. The Other left her with a twenty-dollar gold piece CC 1891 and his name only. He had said he would return. He said he would take her to Paradise, to Echevarria's. Whose woman was she? His?

I just know there's silver dollars in the chest. I just know it! Ever heard of the Redfield hoard?

No, not really.

Some Reno girl you are. La Vere Redfield, eccentric casino mogul, real estate investor and man-in-over-alls-about-town at one time owned most of Washoe County and Lake Tahoe. Kinda like Pete Itçaina in Elko. You heard of *him*?

No, but it sounds Basque. You've noticed I'm, uh, Chinese?

Well that would be the thing to be to get into Cal in the 70s alright. (Sorry, PhD envy). Anyways, Redfield left an estate of over $100 million in 1974. His coal chute was full of one of the biggest hoards of silver dollars in history. Some say his stone mansion on Mt. Rose Street holds more. *Nork dakit?*

Fascinating. Let's excavate it after you finish with that box. Hey, please, be careful!

Kontuz ibilli. Take it easy.

How do you know so much Basque?

I lived in the Basque country, Oñate a mountain-ous inland of Gipuzkoa. That's where Pedro Altube was from. St. Ignatius of Loyola near by . . . You don't know *Pedro Altube?* Go figure. I thought you were a real Nevada historian. Wow, anyways, Oñate was a BSU program for half-breeds like me, Basque-American boy *erdi-purdiz* half-assed *hunzue.*

Time travel vacation? "Roots"?

You goddamnbetchya. Guardia Civil with machine guns on every corner of downtown Bilbao. Demonstrations and rubber bullets for the village crowds. After Franco died all hell broke loose. Good hell though, 70s hell. They say ETA is responsible for a hundred fatalities a year from 1978–80. I don't know, maybe 800–1000 total, *esaten da*, they say.

Sure beats Kent State. The Basques were with the Republic?

Except for Álava and Navarra.

Civil war too? Why were you there? Like Hemingway or what?

Our school was in an abandoned seminary building. There was still a cloistered convent in Oñate in the 70s. The nuns with perfectly unlined skins peeking out at us from the iron grille. It was a real trip! Groov-y. Mainly we went to drink wine and learn Basque (in that order). In the bars during the *txikiteo* villagers stared at our Vasque (funny huh?) hiking boots, the heavy down jackets that functioned miserably in the rain, our long hair and Berkeley and Gonzaga sweat shirts. Ironically enough, they called us "*Nixonista-faxistak*". We, the grandchildren of lowly shepherds and chamber maids, "*cochino capitalistas*", "*La Th-i-a*".

The what?

C.I.A. in Spanish with the "*th*" ceta. I spent a night in Mondragón on a bar floor listening to Benito Lertxundi and Laboa on the jukebox all night under cover. Kinda cool, like 1968 only it was Spain and 1978. Hey, you were at Berkeley in the 60s. It musta rocked.

Rocked 'n rolled.

Did you, were you like, involved in anything?

I lived in Barrington Hall.

Doesn't sound very counterculture.

It used to be the SDS headquarters. I got there late.

Wow, Tom Haydn.

And Jane Fonda. No guardias or bullets at Cal though, just Harry Edwards and Ralph Nader's sister Laura. I had a class from her. At Barrington off Telegraph we had a pet squatter named Pink Cloud. He was a "left-over" from all the ruckus, won the counter-culture revolution, lost his mind. The place smelled like curry, patchouli and backed-up sewage the entire time I lived there.

Persistent odors those. I still dream them.

There, everything's plotted. Now, can we open it, Lily Sue?

Can we open you?

Better turn in and get some shut eye, cowboy. Long day ahead.

Longer night, I hope against hope.

Good night, sweet prince.

Did you say "swee-eet"?

Day 2: Tuscarora

> Elko Daily Free Press, Nov. 3, 1888
> Tuscarora is a lively town, and during the races last week looked more like a small city than a mining camp.
>
> The engine for the Union mill is the heaviest ever shipped to Tuscarora. The fly-wheel shaft alone weighs 6,000 pounds. May 4, 1889: Fourteen bars of Navajo bullion, valued at $21,000, came down from Tuscarora Tuesday evening.
>
> Milt Campbell lost his steel crowbar the other day, while coming in town with a load of wood. It dropped somewhere Chinatown and the brewery. It is pointed at one end and flat at the other. The finder will be treated well by returning it to Milt.

What do you think is in the box? Gold bullion maybe? It's made of metal only part of it's rusted. It's got a lock on it, looks like some kind of strong box like a safe. I bet it was off a stagecoach, you know, like in the Westerns.

We must first delineate the walls, trace the floor plan of the building.

What building?

The one we are excavating. Judging from the chest it is most probably the Tong House.

I don't see any walls.

That doesn't mean they aren't there. *Ngoh sink yeem doh gwoh nay sink mie.*

If you're going to talk about me at least feign the translation.

"I eat salt more than you eat rice."

Say what?

Translation: "I'm your tenure chair".

Be my tenure bed, Suzy Wong.

Who?

"The World of Suzy Wong" 1960. William Holden and Nancy Kuan, Eurasian dancer, who replaced France Nuyen, "South Pacific," the original choice for the film who pigged out after a disastrous affair with asshole Marlon Brando and couldn't fit into a *cheongsam* which Nancy, the model, then made famous via Yves St. Laurent.

Do you have the schemata complete, all the important details?

Sure. Is this a house or a business? How do you know?

There are always clues left to be re-examined. The foundation, detritus, the location of the entrance, structural remains; there is the relative size and relationship of the structure to other contextual structures. Even as scientists we extrapolate our own inner reality upon

the external. We project our *desire* for what we wish
our history to be or especially, to have been.

Desire?

For lack of a better term.

Say it again. I like that word. In French this time.

Get real.

Real as it gets, Babe.

> *Now quiet until tomorrow. The walls so thin. Per-
> haps it was a blessing Wing-Chiu had been sold. It
> had brought money to them a little at least. The last
> of it she would hide from him safe in the pouch for
> Ana's future dowry. She must find a way to trick
> him. He would take it to Paradise, gamble it all
> away. She must find a way of hiding it. Perhaps
> Wing-Chiu would eat better now. A male child
> had a chance at least on Yinshan Silver Mountain.
> Why, old Leong himself they said had been sold as
> a boy in the Virginia City place and how he was
> master, had hoards of gold hidden beneath false
> floorboards they said. She would give offerings,
> burnings tonight for her first son. Red envelopes of
> blessing at the joss house from her secret cache for
> Anastacia Echevarria.*

Maybe you're *not* getting tenure.

Case of sexual harassment? Or doesn't it work both
ways?

I work both ways.

You work every way. All work no play makes Suzy
Q a dull girl.

Dull, then. Safer.

Always risk surprise, Darlin.

Who said *that*?

Candido Goicoechea.

That's you.

That's me, *ogi metako txoria*. Small bird on mountain of crumbs.

Ah! There's one in Chinese exactly like that.

Hey, perfect transliteral communication through proverbs. Who did live here, Doc?

Folks without much. Your people, my people, desperate immigrants with no other options. See the smoke hole?

Where?

There. Probably didn't have window panes. It could get rather dismal in here during a long, hard winter, but then it beat freezing to death.

At least they had a structure. My great uncle Ottio talked about the sheep camps in Copper Canyon before they brought in the wagons. All the herder had as a guarantee for survival was a canvas tent or tarp, a .30-.30 and a dog.

A lot of Basque sheepherders were actually cowboys. And did you know that the All-Around Cowboy of the Silver State Stampede of 1908 was Chinese?

I thought you didn't know any Basque-American-Chinese history.

I looked it up, because of the Chinese connection.

Did *you* know Mrs. C.G. Chang neé Wang had bound feet in Carson City in 1906? I looked it up because of—

Spare me the details. I think I know the your, uh, impetus.

Good word for it. One fact is certain.

And what is that?

You and me *kuli*, people at hard labor. You makin me work hard in hot sun, Boss Lady.

Dahn yeun dzie. Mm yeu who seung.

I'm not even gunna ask. It's all Greek Chinese to me.

It looks like a single room.

How do you know?

No wall demarcations. It's so small. A dwelling directly connected to a stable.

Like in the Basque farmstead *baserri*. But here the people are inside with the animals?

If they were lucky enough to have animals.

How did an entire family live in here? It's so cramped.

They lived uncomfortably, miserably.

Hey, why are there no floorboards left?

There never were any.

It was just dirt? People lived in dirt?

The woman of the house would wet it down good then sweep it. It formed a kind of clay, earth linoleum.

But if it rained or snowed. . .

> *To keep them above the ground keep them silent. What good is the girl child but for suckling, mewing and pissing? He had told her what they should have done. Now a big squawking thing with the odd eyes, hunxue. It was difficult to snuff out life so over grown now. How has she gotten fat on such food then? You hide something from me, woman! The One had come again and the woman was pregnant.*

Who the hell lived like this?

The Chinese in the West mainly. Not exactly your white bread John Wayne Western?

John Ford, puleeze. What about your *Good Earth*? *The Good Earth*, 1937. Paul Muni as Wang Lung, wasn't

even Chinese. Pearl S. Buck, you know, Nobel Prize?
You a movie buff?

Sort of. You?

Only movies before 1960. Ever see *Thunder in the
Sun*? 1959, Susan Hayward and Jeff Chandler. It's ridiculous! They used *txisterak* as weapons and shouted
irrintzi ululations as meaningful communication. I'm
a regular ciné-assed, case you hadn noticed.

What's a *txistera*?

Show ya later, Lady.

You have one? Here?

Indeed, I do.

You walkin on thin waters, Grasshopper.

Walking on *waters*? Mixed metaphor or Freudian,
Miz post-Doc? I think that's thin *ice*, ain't it? God, I'm
getting drunk. You?

That *irrintxi* thang then? What is it? You gonna
take it out?

You had to ask. It is a rapid movement of tongue
and uvula. We Basques are quite good at it. Wanna see?

I'll save the trill for later. *Aieeeeee ya ha ha ha ha!!!*
What is the, uh, origin of this *irintzi* ululation?

A universal song of happiness originating from
shepherds produced by rapidly moving the tongue,
back and forth in the mouth while producing a sharp
sound. A war cry.

AieeeeeeeeeeeeYiiiiiiiaaaaah....

My, my. Fan-cy.

It's apocryphal that it's just Basque. You can find
it in Palestine, Persia, Sub-Saharan Africa. Egypt,
Greece—any place ya got a shepherd which used to be
every place.

You may just get that PhD after all depending. Pass
the Jack, Daniels.

Ofera. Off to bed with you, Suzy Q.

There are no beds.

Let's go to sleeping bag then. Like all Basque herders and conquistadores. To bed roll we go! *Couchez-vous* you. I mean *nous on cochons.*

'm gonna stay out here and read the Free Press by the fire, if it's all the same to you.

It's not and that paper's over a week old. Ancient history.

Better old news than no news.

> *American woman! / Stay away from mee . . . ee /*
> *American woman, / Mama let me bee...ee.*

Don't you ever give up?

> *Now wo-man, I said / Get a-waa-uhy / Listen*
> *what I say-uhya / Don't come hanging / Round*
> *my tent / Don't wanna see your face all bent.*

Shut the fuck up, Can-di-do.

Oh Suzy Q / Baby, I love you / Say / you'll be true . . .
Suzy Q

Day 3: *June 1982*

There. Everything's plotted and accounted for. Now, can we open it? Come on, it's probably nothing at all: old letters, toys, junk. Did you see it's made of metal only part of it's rusted? It's got a lock on it. It looks so common, not much like a treasure box.

Depends on whose treasure. It is however somewhat unusual for this type of building.

What building? Nothing's left.

It is a dwelling.

I don't see any walls.

That doesn't mean that there weren't any. *Ngahng gayng.*

You called me something not good.

How ever would you know?

Tone. Tone of voice. It wasn't nice. Even dogs know.

Sorry. I have a migraine. Too much Jack last night.

Who lived in these box shanties? Was it like in the movies?

Chinese lived here and Paiute, Shoshone, Mexicans, a widow with a pack of dysenterried kids. Over there at the "boardinghouse" maybe a miner with a busted leg no good for work, an alcoholic mule driver out of a job, a prostitute or two.

Were there any gunslingers? Maybe we'll find a six shooter. My great-uncle Ottio had a .30-.30 and he knew how to use it. That, at least is a fact.

They had rifles and pistols and knives and crow bars. My great-uncle was beaten to death with a crowbar in a back alley of Paradise. No guarantees. It was usually a little more brutal than pacing off ten steps on Main Street at high noon. More like a bullet in the back, a blow to the head while you slept. A festering wound was more likely in the wild, wild West, a long bout of pneumonia, infection. Some starved. Many of our people ignored by the histories died slowly, too slowly. In the end, the human body is actually excruciatingly resilient.

Did the Indians shoot bows and arrows? I mean the Paiutes didn't, right?

The Shoshone and Paiute, Ute tribes, were hunter gatherers not like the Plains warriors of your Westerns. The Know Nothings wiped them out by slow attrition with their forts, the relocations to colonies, then by the infamous Ruby Mountain treaty for which the natives had no concept of law. By the twentieth century they'd been sent to reservations mostly or used as slave labor on ranches, in mines, as servants to the dominant culture like our people.

But the Basques made it. The governor of Nevada was Reagan's best friend and considered a presidential candidate! His father was a sheepherder. You ever read *Sweet Promised Land*? Laxalts sure made it. What's the dif?

Skin. And eyes. Not Sino-Mongoloid. Not Asiatic.

But Indians aren't Asian.

Aren't they? As the black "Negro" would say of the "Yella": You Basques passed.

> The Reno Evening Gazette,
> June 18, 1913
>
> Nearly all of the laborers employed in (the sheepherding) occupation are Basque sheep herders, who can hardly speak the English language, and get about $35 a month. The Basques come from the Pyrenees mountains in Spain. (The sheep men) get that class of labor because they seem to be adapted for sheep herding, and they are lacking in intelligence, independence, or anything else. They are just about as near a slave as anybody could be under our present existing conditions. As a general thing they never associate with other people in the state. They live among themselves; they can only speak a few words of the English language; they live in the lowest possible way for a human being to live; and they are nothing but sheepherders. Senator Key Pittman, 1913.

Barely passed.

We both be *kuli*.

Precisely. It is estimated that workers from South China made up more than 90 percent of the workforce of some 15,000 men who laid the rails west. Thousands upon thousands perished. The tracks of the Central Pacific were laid on the backs of 5,000 Chinese.

The Chinese Exclusion Acts beginning as early as the 1880s were really about prohibiting citizenship and land ownership. After the railroads were built, some opened restaurants on land leased from the railroad to serve the traveling public.

Like the Basque, the problem for the Chinese *was* their hard work, persistence and thrift: their own virtue and success as citizens! Since traditionally they valued the ownership of land, the 1861 Nevada Constitution lured Chinese associations and wealthy Chinese from California and elsewhere to "stake their claims", typically played out mining claim sold to them by Euro American miners. After the railroads were built, some opened restaurants on land leased from the railroad to serve the traveling public. Chop Suey was the Chinese gold, and laundry.

The gold on The Mountain is reserved for the dominant culture, even if it is the *kuli* who works it from the dirt. This is true as true of Spain in the New World as it is of the Old World. It is labor which builds empires. Fortune is loaded on the backs of the mule-peasant. For the lord of the manor, for the king. Even virtue is converted to vice.

Will all this be on the final?

We *kuli*, you and me. Just call us "shit labor."

Hey, I think you and me got *guanxi* together, Doctor.

The Caldwell Tribune, July 17, 1909

The sheep men of the Owyhee county are sorely beset by Biscayans ... and trouble may result most any time. The wool growers themselves introduced the Biscayans into this country and instructed them in the sheep business, because they could get them for a smaller wage. The business practices and culture of the Bascos are on par with those of the Chinaman, but The Chinaman was not filthy, treacherous and meddlesome like the clannish and undesirable Basque who make life impossible for the white man.

CHINESE
NEP SUEY or SUEY
DIED IN A SNOWSTORM
JUNE 20, 1897
AGE 52 YEARS

They say you're separated.

Just conflicted.

I mean from your husband.

Zai zi. Past history.

Isn't it Yogi Berra who said "The future ain't the way it used to be"?

Speaking of the future, you ready for your exams?

Affirmative. I'm gunna *pass* for white this time.

Tant mieux. It's your last chance, cowboy.

When I pass next May, I'm gonna buy you a lamb steak and a picon punch, my lady, at famous Echevarrias Steakhouse & Saloon.

End of Days: Reno, June 1983

One year later come spring, Dr. Chang, née Wong, prepared for the Cortez dig with Dr. Donald Hardesty, chair of the departments of anthropology and archeology at the University of Nevada, Reno. Grad Assistant, Candido Goicoechea, she had learned, would not be with them on the excavation party this year. Dr. Chang, aka: Lily Susan, unrolled her last summer's sleeping bag in preparation for the new dig and discovered the one artifact that would become the most important find of her life—a Sony Walkman complete with a single cassette tape for which she now needed no translation.

My Sweet Hometown Girl

Ahozko lorez zaitut gaur laztantzen
itxaso garden, lur gozoko landare
kresalaren usain, zeru kolore.

Nere biotzaren taupaden hotsez
zure grazia dut kantatzen.
Nere biotzaren taupaden hotsez
zure grazia dut kantatzen...

Bihotz minberen egunsentia
herri sufrituaren lamia.

Ipuin zaharren, piper eta eztia,
erreka garbien kantu bitxia.

Udazken lizunez zaude jantzia,

izar zerutarren irria.
Udazken lizunez zaude jantzia
izar zerutarren irria. . .

Lanbro artetik itsas geldira
Like a bird in flight joyous
leunki zoazen txori airosa
Amodiozko sentipenaren hatsa.

Zure ezpainetan loratuz doa
goizeko ihintzetan belardi zera, (You are)
eguzkitan zilar dizdira. (the morning dawn)
      Goizeko ihintzetan belardi zera (the
brilliance of silver in the sun)
      eguzkitan zilar dizdira . . . (you are)

1992
Chino

Los güeros son muy maloras,
Se valen de la occasion,
Y a todos los mexicanos, nos tratan
Sin compassion . . . venimos a camellar

Papi died on Tuesday. It was his liver they said. Some people say it was his heart, *sufría del corazón*. We don't know for sure cause he never went to the doctor and we can't afford an autopsy (that's when they cut you up and take the heart and stuff out like the Aztecs did). They planted him good in the ground today after the funeral alright. My teacher came and all the waitresses too. They had a party at Echevarrias and my *tíos* from Bakersfield all got drunk. They work the fields until their visas run out, then they come back with a *coyote*. Tía Dolores, the sister of Mamá, died in a van coming across. They was all dead and rotting, twelve of em and Papi's primo from Guadalajara. They already paid their money, five hundred *dólares* each, and the coyote wouldn't give it back to their families. That'd be most of a month's *sueldo* for us and we work from eight in the morning until closing, with a party until midnight. (She takes out a lot for our room and food).

I wash dishes after school and on weekends. Mamá and Papi don't get extra *sueldo* for me and Teresita. That's cause La Patrona says it's against the American law to pay kids for work and Mamá and Papi are illegals. Only I maybe can get papers because of Indiano. He said the priest could work it out "with a bowl of pasta". Then I could work outside or fight for the military with benefits and Mamá could rest. *Es mi sueño,* that's my dream. I wonder if Papi got legal up in heaven finally. Maybe the priest got him in with a *pago* too. What kinda papers you need any way? Probably the baptism and I'm sure he had that so he's good to go. I don't think you gotta have last rites no more, but what would I know? I'm just a kid and a Mexican. Teresita was baptized in Méjico. I wonder if that counts for anything here? I know I'm in cause Father Joe did it to me when I was little right here in Paradise. Aita Indiano *es mi padrino*, my guardian angel father with wings. I got his back too cause he's old and not a sheeper no more. He says if he didn't have a gun people would rob all his "pelas" (that means money to him). No one knows if he's really got the pasta, only maybe Bob Goicoechea that's his lie-yer. "*Ya veremos*", says La Patrona. I guess we'll just have to wait and see.

Teresita (thas my sister) isn't as lucky as me cause she's a girl. She was born in Méjico anyway—an illegal. She's real tall and skinny and weird lookin'. She's supposed to wear glasses so she's always scrunching up her face funny like a conejo, ya know? To bug her I call her "conejita", funny little bunny. That makes her real mad and she pounds on me good, but it's worth it. Mamá's afraid of her seeing boys cause she'll get a baby. (Good thing she's ugly, I say). When Mamá had me La Patrona got all mad cause she said we couldn't support any more kids, so she paid to have Mamá fixed like Americans do their poodles. They cut off all her tubes and she got real skinny and yellow. Mamá's Católica. She thinks God will punish her for it. That's why she lights so many candles because of Papi too. Tío Mariano is taking us out to The Steakhouse after the service which is really "in" cause that's where we live and work 24/7 at Echevarria.

The sign outside on Main Street says our place is "Echevarria", but nobody can remember why and my teacher says it should have an apostrophe somewhere or an "s", but everybody calls it "The Steakhouse" anyway. Tío Mariano said we must be *como perros*, hungry as dogs. It's so weird to eat here like a customer at a table. We always eat in the kitchen, usually standing up. Mamá never eats any more anyway. That's weird too cause we can eat all the meat scraps we want off people's plates. If you're lucky you can get a piece a chicken or shrimps from kids or old ladies. When she's not in the kitchen Papi cooks what he wants anyway, only sometimes you gotta stuff it in your mouth real fast. I save the left-over shrimps for Teresita or Mamá. We've got a room upstairs too only there's no pictures or rugs like a real house. Papi always said we were here solo para un rato, then we were going back to Guadalajara where his family had land and we were somebody gente de algo—that was twenty years ago, I guess. Late at night Mamá used to whisper to us in the dark about Zacatecas, that's Guadalajara. I guess that's where we're from. ¡*Aie Ama*! she'd always say. "*Las catedrales, las frutas tropicales, paletas de piñón!*

Aie, las mariachis, las flores!" She don whisper this to
me at night no more. I guess she just got tired of her
dreams. Anyway Papi, he finally got the flowers at the
Rosario last night and a priest too. It was like *navi-
dades* and Easter all stuck together. It was real nice. No
Santa or bunny though, no candy. The church as dark
and quiet, everybody mumblin prayers—the candle-
light and yellow shadows, the smell a wax and tea tree
oil. The priests were in their silvery robes moving like
moonlight, hoverin hawks over the coffin. (Thas the
best part). Don Ernesto, her final husband, is the only
other dead person I know besides Papi.

Don Ernie liked sheepherding (not like Ottio
Indiano). I dunno if he likes town all that much, but
she kept him here alright, it was where the money was.
They say he dropped dead in the shower of a heartache
or something, some kinda disattach of his aorta. Papi
said Don Ernie's eyes turned black like stones when he
died. I dunno. He was all stiff and hard like an old bull
Papi seen once all frozen up solid back in the cow pasture that hard winter when I was three. He was known
for his eyes. The eyes were light blue like the sun, the
eyebrows black and bushy like dead caterpillars rising
laying still there across his forehead in the grass: he was
my first dead man, Mister.

I used to wanna be a priest only they don't get to
play baseball or nothing. They get all their food though,
and a house and car for free. Old church ladies invite
em to dinner all the time, and in Nevada they get to
play the slots machines! One priest I know got his own
pandemonium when a guy died and left it to him in his
will. He still lives there for free. Anyways, now I don't
think the vows are quite worth it. You're givin up a lot
of good stuff, ya know. Indiano says he don't believe in

no church. He says man made church, God made the sky. He'll talk to God outside thank you very mucho. I want to be a writer like Jack London. He's my favorite author. My teacher says I'm pre-co-cious. I just like to read books a lot, especially adventures. Jack London loves Alaska and dogs and stuff just like me. If you're a sheepherder or a cowboy (I don't know if they let Indians be) out here on the frontier you got to have a .30.30, a horse and a dog minimum. *¿Verdad que sí?*

Jack London's aways got a dog in his story. Thas why he's my favorite. It's all about the call a the wild, ya know? Only we can't have a dog at Echevarrias. We live upstairs, there's no yard to play or anything. I dreamed a border collie that was mine once though. A black and white one. I pitched a tent in the mountains and she came right in. She snuffled my neck and started gnawin on my shirt cuffs. It was nice that dream. I've had it again. I think I'll really come to see her, that dog, ya know? The one that's really mine. Don Ernesto, La Patrona's last husband, liked dogs a lot too. Papi gave him the name Don Ernesto. I think he liked it—it fit. Him and Papi liked dogs too even though we couldn't have one. Once drinking whiskey (or tequila if my Papi was with them) out behind the shed in the cow pasture shed they ate grass after to cover up the smell, only it made their teeth all green and she found out. It was real funny! That was before Papi went to prison for his fourth drive-n-drinkin DUIs and Don Ernie dropped dead just like that. There was real hell to pay and Papi had to pay her back with his life, Mamá said, just like the time when I was born in the American hospital. It costs a lot to be born here and even more to die, ya know. In Mexico life is cheap so it doesn't cost as much to live or even die. I don't know about the dying part here either, but I'm real worried. It all looks so pricey. It'll take us years to pay her off again.

Hoy es el entierro. They always have a big meal after the funeral so lotsa people'll come. Everybody's looking at us like we got the wrong clothes on cause we're jus Messicans. *"Meshikanoak"*, Indiano calls us only he says it all soft-like because he says he's *"Meshikano"* too now that I'm his son. I dunno, I don't understand it all. I bet La Patrona gets all his money anyways somehow. She's been waiting for him to kick the bucket for about twenty years. Ha! Now he's almost a hundred! Darla, the main Echevarria waitress now, keeps patting me on the top of the head like a mangled puppy. I guess she's never seen me sitting down before. People act weird when your Papi's dead. Tío Mariano says he's paying, but Mamá looks worried. Everybody knows he's got money cause a the settlement from the mines for his crushed leg. That's the good thing about America though, if you can get disabled without getting killed you can get money for it. Tío Mariano said they used to do it on the railroad, even the highway all the time. Thas cause if you're illegal, he says, *solo es cuestión de tiempo.* I guess that's pretty much true for everybody though, ya know? He eats in restaurants almost every day, only they say he doesn't give his wife anything now that he's rich and they have five kids. She can't get child supports because he's not a citizen. Everybody's got it bad sometimes, just in their own way.

None of the outside people knows how to order so Tío Mariano gets shrimps for the women and steak for the men. Tío Mariano pours Mamá some more wine. He's the head of our family now, I guess. She never drinks, but he insists. Her black dress hangs like a big, black sack on her. *Siento vergüenza,* I feel shame, she

says. She looks so shrunken, her head bowed down
over her plate like in church, all sad like La Sagrada
Corazón. Tío Juanito tells a dirty joke and everybody
laughs too loud. (Ottio Indiano next to him looks like
he's gonna pop a gut. Looks just like he does when he
squeezes the trigger on his pistol). My soup looks like
white snakes swimming in piss. *Aie Angula!* I can't eat
it. My good shoes hurt my feet bad cause they're way
too small, anyway. Tío Mariano orders another bottle
of wine. He keeps rubbing Mamá's arm. I don't like
the looks of it. I won't ever drink alcohol unless I'm a
priest then you have to drink wine because it's sacrifi-
cial. Papi used to say he took wine *para los nervios,* for
the cold in his bones, for high blood pressure, because
he was a drunk! He looked so funny in the casket like
plastic or rubber or something. It looked like Papi, but
not like Papi, ya know?

Maybe I killed Papi since I prayed to eat at the banquet table one day. He had a nice funeral. There was even
a big wreath of red roses like at the end of the horse rac-
es. Tía Concha says all the dead people get the ring (all
the Mexicans give money) and Papi got a Spanish priest
from Fresno too cause Papi was real good to people.
He was a real *don de gente*, that's what Tía Concha says
anyway. My Papi's "*don de gente*" got to be a joke after
a while so many people saying it so he started to call
himself "don Gente", so it caught on. I was real worried
someone was gonna put that on the tombstone ("Don
de Gente"). It's a joke if you know Spanish. "Don", get
it? I guess it don't work quite in English.

Where Don Ernie really made his money was in
slot machines. Don Ernie and La Patrona would stand
all day watching the machines and knew when they'd
hit to play em themselves, ya know? Don Ernie knew

an old guy named Dick Graves whose wife was Vizcaína
from Idaho built the Carson and Sparks Nugget Casinos, sold him his first quarter machines for Echevarrias
until he moved to dollars. Boy was that a good move!
Indiano says he's still young. He's only *laurogei urte
gainena ditut.* I'd guess at least a hundred. That'll be
good in your book, mister. I think he still dreams about
getting home and seeing the look on that Marie's face
when he shows her his black book. It's got all his money in it. It's called "Passbook Savings", I guess that's it.
He says he's had it since 1932. He says it will be mine
when he dies, not for Teresita. He never pays attention to Teresa. He likes me best cause I'm a boy. They
all call me "Chino" not cause I'm Chinese or nothing.
(I bet you thought that), but cause a my eye slants.
Soy Totonaco. Puro Indio! That's what Papi used to say.
We're pure Indian. Garcia y Vasquez alright, gente de
algo you goddamnbetchya! (You know we don't know
exactly who my Dad is, right, Mister?)

La Patrona thinks Indiano's got hoards of money
hidden though. That's why Patrona keeps him, they
say. Indiano says if he ever looks like he's ready to die I
should do two things: one, drag him out on the street so
he doesn't croak in this nogoodgoddamnittohellwom-
enspissplace, and two: grab the black book that belongs
to Nebada Nacional Banco de Comercio and go to Bob
Goicoechea that Basco lawyer on Main Street *echando
chispas!* (That means right away). *Ez esan ezer inori.* Don't
talk to no-bo-dy! he says. (I guess that's three things).

The steak comes rare on my plate dropped in a pud-
dle of blood. Tío Mariano glares at me cause he's paying. The money's not worth his stupid foot anyways.
Teresita looks down her nose at me all squinty only I
know she's faking it. Girls always fake it, that's what

Inazio says. (*He should know, Putasemea*). That's what
Indiano always says about Inazio. Maybe Papi just
got some bad meat like the cats. Mamá says all the
Americanos smell like meat. They sweat it out their
puffy bodies like pigs, their skin all white and pinkish,
güero-cochinos, Mamá always says. (I know this is true
cause Father O'Connor kissed me once after a funeral
in the sacristy and his wet, red lips tasted real sour like
old meat and wine).

Tío Mariano orders another bottle of wine. (Maybe
Papi was right about el vino veritas). My bones
feel all warm and mushy inside my skin, nice. Stupid
Teresita's having a good time. She forgets to act sad
with her black lace party dress from the second-hand
store. Everybody's looking down at my steak and me,
I can't eat it. All I can think about is the big brown and
white cow they killed for me. I like cows a lot so I want
to be a vegetarian. Don Ernesto used to have some out
back in the field, only she said they made too much
noise when their milk bags were full so she butchered
em. I found one of the cats dead in the lettuce in the
dumpsters once: a big, yellow tabby. We all knew it
was Teresita's baby cause she called him "Pepo" and
made a bed of potato sacks under the back stairs for
him. I don't like cats as much as dogs and horses. They
just don't make for good stories, ya know? Pepo was
all right though, kinda a doggish cat. He'd follow you
all around Echevarrias and would meow like a watch
cat to warn us Papi was coming up the stairs. (That
was handy alright). After I found him all dead like
that, Teresita said he wasn't hers anyway and that
she hated animals. Girls pretend a lot. They have to or
their men will hit em around and leave em with lotsa
kids. Everybody's finishing their steaks and shrimps

except for me. Teresita is pretending again she's sad about Papi only she's really thinking how she can sleep with Mamá again in her own bed. It scared her when he used to come in *tomado* so late at night. ¡*Aie Conejita!* Little rabbit, little one. Teresa's in high school now. La Patrona says Teresa'll never make Steak House waitress cause she's a puta whore. Papi hit her hard across the face cause she snuck off with Carlitos her novio on her birthday. (I think she really did it with him that time).

Darla takes away the big steak platters and brings coffee. All I can think about is all those dishes to wash: soup bowl, salad plate, dinner plate, cup, saucer, water glass, wine glass, steak platter, cream pitcher, sugar bowl, ice cream cup, side plate, ashtray, knife, fork and spoon, ashtray. *Bebe hombre, bebé!* Drink little baby, drink! (Tío Mariano's always joking like that) I got a pretty good priest story if you got time, only there's never bullets or dogs in priest stories. They die sometimes, it's just not a big deal since they know where they're going. For them, it's all guaranteed. I wonder if dogs know, you know, whether they're going to die or not. Lucky if they don't, huh? Papi used to call death "*la perra negra*", the black bitch. I wonder if she came for him or for Don Ernie since his eyes were so black frozen in his head? *Nork dakit?* Who knows? Maybe Bob Goicoechea. He's got the Jesuit education!

We got to get done with this funeral thing. La Patrona's looking down at the top of my head glaring at my untouched steak. I hate meat. You don't have to eat it if you're católica really, only fake bread wafers, la hostia, host (only it's not real meat just a pla-ce-bo) and you get to eat nothing good during Lent! Teresita is

greedily sucking dry the little paper cup of red sauce
from her shrimps where it leaves a red stain and I hav-
en't even touched my steak. Mamá sits still, her small
brown hands shaking. Her head looks all black and
wrinkled up like a shrunken head. *Aie Sandunga, Sandunga Mamá de Dios.* . . *A-díos,* she says to people, her
tight, black bun at her neck like a noose. So silent. *Qui-
eta.* Still, like our black Virgen de Guadalupe.

   Grateful, grateful. We are so very grateful for such
a nice funeral. And Papi would turn away in shame,
his black eyes like a coward bow down *como un buey*
an oxen yoked, he'd say, *Soy como un buey.* We say,
Muchísimas gracias for everything para todo." The long
white neck craned over me looking at my meat. Those
vampire lips in the pale, white face. Steak. Steak. Lamb
steak, beef steak. Everybody wants steak. Everybody
watching me waiting to eat it. Go down Moses! O
Sweet Promised Land!

   Mamá, nervous all seriosa, mumbling her mother's
rosario clacking the beads like pieces of bone. La Patrona
squints hard, her white apron belly breathing tight up
and down up and down. She smiles her customer smile
now impatient, pats my head like a little dog. *"He's too
young too young to understand. If he doesn't want to eat a
perfectly good steak, what can we do? Too young. Without
meat he will always be weak. La carne, la carne da vida."*
Meat is life-giving. Meat is for the living.

   I understand plenty. I understand I'm not gonna
get knocked across the head any more when he comes
up the stairs dead drunk. I understand his black eyes
growling are shut tight in that big, black box forever.
¡*Cabrón! ¡ Melolengua! Bastard, idiot! Bebé. ¡Niñita! ¡Tu
puta madre!"* Your black whore mother! *Just a little
boy with a big man's steak. That's why he can't eat it.*

¡Cabrón! my uncle hisses beneath his breath. Big and white she presses her big belly into my chin. *Madre de Díos,* she pokes the point of the steak knife like a butcher into my meat—the arm huge hard against me, her armpit bitter: lemon soap, garlic, vinegar. My uncle's eyebrows raise like black crows above the coal dark eyes. The steak. Steak. The meat. La carne de La Incarnacíon. Lamb of God who takes away the sins of the world, have mercy on us. Cordero de Dios. This is my body that was given for you. Have mercy on us.

The customers in the main dining are stuffed: their gray-white heads bobbing, their bodies obese. In the end they must pay: *Mastercar, Bisa or Americanespress?* La Patrona Americana strolls off to her cash register, her customer smile ready. She rings up the check, then pats the green bills to sleep in the big, black box—deep deep so much money *tantos billetes* to sleep. *Muy agradecidos. Come mihijo.* Eat. Eat my son. This is my body. Such a nice meal. *Agradecidos muy* grateful. Mamá, her small, brown hands now quivering. *Aie Mamá. No puedo.*

Muchísimas gracias, real grateful, she shaking.

Bebe bebé, drink little man, drink. This is my blood.

¡Cabrón melolengua! little bastard, all the family relations, *Enano.*

¡Bebé! hisses Mariano, black-eyed saint of the broken foot.

Mijo, pobrecito. My son, my poor one. What have I done?

Mamá mamá. No puedo. Ni para tí can't eat this meat la *carne para tí.* Meat red meat on a clean white plate. Meat fat bloodied like a liver. Meat like th heart of la *Mamá de mi corazón.*

¡*Idiota*! hisses Teresita *conejita*, little rabbit caught in her own wire trap. Her beady bald eyes squeeze hard against the tears. *I'll never be steak house waitress now.*

Hemen gire
Etorri geralako

We are here
Because we have come

Akerra ken ken
The goat has come
to eat the wheat

Otsua
The wolf
to eat the goat

Zakurra
The dog is always with us

I am Ramon

Law Office Center
Goicoechea, DiGrazia & Stanton, Ltd.

- Robert B. Goicoechea -
ATTORNEY AT LAW

Ph 775-738-8091
Fax 775-738-4220
www.lawyers.com/elklaw

P.O. Box 1358
530 Idaho Street
Elko, Nevada 89801

Spanish Ranch
1902

Vaquero Castro	Joe Shorty Johnson
Chappo the Milker	Al Shannon
Juan Rios	Ramon Lugea the Blacksmith
Charley Galinda	Pat the Chinese Cook
Tio Achile	Joe the Vaquero Cook
Lolo Montez	Jose Urias
Pete Porcupine Martinez	Ben Loines
Chris Aguilar	Francisco Goicoechea
Chappo Viejo	Joe Yraguen
Pete Orbe	Jose Sustacha
Jim Chick-a-Biddy Tunnell	
	Pedro & Bernardo Altube
	Felix & Jules

Nevada State Herald: August 11, 1905.
Pedro Altube, the Independence stockman died in San Francisco Tuesday.
During the past three years he has
been in poor health and his death was
not unexpected. Since the 1870s he
has been a resident of Elko County. An
aged wife and four married daughters
survive him. The enormous estate will
pass to his wife, Marie.

Star Hotel
2002

Hey, son-of-a-bitch, my friend, take a drink
with me
Aieeeiiiiíieeehahaha! EHH éé yiiiii iiieeeEE!

Can I talk to him now?
He doesn't talk any more.
I've come all the way from Europe to talk to him.
We're from Euzkal Telebista, boy.
It's cause he's 'The Last Basque Sheepherder', huh?
Maybe. ¿Hablas español, muchacho? ¿Mejicano?
I no speak Spanish. Me American boy. I only un-
derstand.
(*Txori buru*) dolt, the cineaste said under his breath.
Euskera egiten dut. I do speak Basque though. You
movie guys gonna eat dinner, mister?

> BASQUE-STYLED-DINNER
> SERVED IN A FAMILY SETTING

INCLUDED WITH ALL ENTREES
Homemade soup, Tossed green salad with Star
Hotel house dressing , Fresh Baked French Bread,
Basque Beans, Pasta, Vegetable Dish, French Fried
Potatoes, Coffee or Tea. Baked Potato . . . .
Tomato Vinaigrette . . . . . .
Sauteed Mushrooms . . . .

(He's my Dad.)
Who is?
Indiano.
What's his Christian, his surname?
No one knows. He lost it.
He lost it?
He's blind, deaf too.
A real TV star, eh? Are there any others? Artzaiñak?
Any sheepherders left? You by chance a vaquero ?

Maybe I should interview you, barman, the first
Basque-Totonaco cowboy in Nevada. What's your real
name, Chino?

Juan Pedro Vasquez. Half Basque, half puro Indio.
Call it a Mexican.

When did you come to this country?
Por aquí paso el 16 de abril de 1605.
Joder.
We don't say that in Mexico, Mister.
When do you think we can film, you know the. . .
end? (Yesterday?)

SCENE 1: TAKE 2

So, who is this Indiano? The last Basque sheepherder?
Véte a saber. (Maybe he's a Messican .)
Seriously, do you know his real name?

Sometime he goes by Enneko, hell if I know.

Elko Free Press: May 1, 1944 To al-
leviate the serious shortage of
sheepherders in Nevada, D. A. Hughes,
secretary-treasurer of the Eastern
Nevada Sheep Growers' Association
and Pete Elia, Elko county sheepman,
left by plane from Salt Lake City last
week for Mexico to secure 100 Basque
herders. Permission was granted by
the immigration service, and approved
by various governmental departments
to recruit 100 Basque refuges now in
Mexico and Latin American countries,
who had escaped from Spain during the
revolution. Under the plan 100 Basque
herders will be brought to Nevada under $500 bond each to guarantee their
departure one year after the close of
the war, as they are being admitted for
the duration of the war and one year
thereafter only.

Bertrand Indiano
DIED
Jan 19, 1911
Age 35 years

Slavery in the West: The Untold Story of the Slavery of Native American
in the West,: It was a day or two later, near the eve of January 1911, when
the three Basque shepherds, John Lax-
ague, Pewter Erramouspe, Bertrand
Indiano with Henry Camron (a cattle-
man) came riding into High Rock Canyon. They rode up to the camp rather
fast and surrounded Mike's camp. He
said that they were guilty of rus-
tling cattle and that they were going
to get some value from them. Two of the
Basque shepherds rushed up on Toad
and grabbed her, one held her arms behind her back while the others began
to tear her dress open.

Cut! Some background information on his time in
Nevada? Was it really seventy years?

Creo que sí.

How many years at Echevarria's?

Thirty maybe.

Thirty? *¡Coño!* What does he talk about?

Not much.

What did he used to talk about?

Dogs.

Anything else?

Saving money.

How about his early life?

One

PYRENEAN CHILDHOOD

I was born in 1888 in Lasse, a little town in the French Basque country. It's right near the border, just a few kilometers from Spain. We were seven brothers and sisters, four boys and three girls, and we lived on a farm called *Gesanburukoborda*.[1]

That place belonged to my grandfather, my mother's father. He was a stonemason when he bought it. My mother and her three brothers grew up there, but then two brothers left for Argentina. The other one went to the army. He came home for a visit and decided not to go back. Instead he deserted and crossed over the border to Spain.[2] So after grandfather died my mother was all alone on that farm. I don't know how she ran it; she just got a little help from the neighbors. But then she married my father. He was from Arneguy and he came to live on *Gesanburukoborda*.

That farm was awfully small, even for the Basque country, so we were very poor. We raised a few pigs and cows and grew a little wheat, corn, and hay. We had some sheep, maybe three hundred head; it was a big bunch for that country. You didn't have to have your own land for the sheep. In the summer they stayed in the mountains and in the winter Father leased fields from the neighbors.[3] Most of the neighbors didn't keep any sheep and after the harvest they didn't need those fields. So Father paid them a little for the stubble and the sheep left manure behind, too.

When I was seven years old I started school, but after about one month some neighbors asked my father if I could go to work for them. Their children were all grown and gone and they couldn't afford a hired man, so they asked my father to send me there. We had a big family already, too many kids, and Father wanted to do them a favor. He sent me there to live.[4] They had a few sheep, maybe twenty-five or fifty. I had to take them to the field in the morning and bring them back at night. They had two or three cows, too, and my job was to move them from one pasture to another.

A young girl, maybe eighteen years old, was living there, just like me, to help out. She did housework and milked the sheep. I took care of the cows, but I was too young to milk them. She was working for wages. I didn't get any money, just my board and some clothes. But they always treated me well, like their own child. I had to stay right there most of the time so I couldn't go to school much. I don't think I ever went more than two months in one year. Altogether I had maybe one year of school.

When I was nine I started catechism. That woman used to send me twice a week to town to the priest. It was like school and I learned to read a little bit that way. I liked catechism because there were lots of other boys and afterwards we could play *pilota* (handball) for maybe half an hour before we had to go home. That was the only chance I had to play because there weren't any other children around our place.

Four or five months before I was eleven I went home to my parents to get ready for my First Communion. After that I stayed right there. They didn't send me back to the other farm. After you made your First Communion you were expected to do a man's work. I stayed home with Father and he taught me all the different jobs. Soon I was strong enough to plow. Most of the work was all by hand. We had to weed the fields with hoes. I learned to use a scythe, too. I cut hay in the fields and ferns in the mountains. We used the ferns for bedding in the stable. I was pretty skinny but I was tall. I had a man's body and my father thought I could do everything, so I had to work very hard.

Right near our place there was an old empty house and everyone said it belonged to the *sorgiñak* (witches).[5] Once my mother's brother went to help some neighbors in their vineyard. That evening he stayed to eat a big supper and then drank lots of wine, so he was coming home pretty late. Well the hour for the witches is between eleven and one at night, and it must have been about that time.

He was pretty happy and he walked along balancing his hoe on his shoulder without using his hands. Then he came to the crossroads where one path went to our place and the other to that old house. Right there he began to fool around. He shouted, "Come here *sorgiña*, I fix you right now." And he took that hoe and began chopping the hard ground on the road. The wine was helping him.

Just then a black cat jumped up on the rock fence along the road. He saw that cat in the moonlight and that scared him. He threw his hoe and the cat screamed. He went over there but he couldn't find a cat or anything. The next day he heard that one old woman that everyone thought was a witch had a broken arm. They say those witches can be cats when they want to go out at night.[6]

When I was about fourteen I started going around with girls a little bit, but I was too young for that so I was pretty shy. The patron saint of our town was Saint Martin and on his feast day there was a big dance in the main plaza. Actually, that was more for the people who lived in the lower part of Lasse, or what we called *Herri Beherekoa*. My house belonged to the upper town, or *Gaineko Plaza,* and on Sunday after Saint Martin's we had our own dance.[7] People came from outside Lasse, like from Luzaire on the Spanish side of the border. Then when there was a fiesta in their town they invited you.

Anyway, there was a girl working for our next-door neighbor and she was from a place called Ondarla that was right on the border. Her father's house was called *Julianenea*, which means "Julian's place." She was about my age. In those days they used cows to pull the plow and somebody had to lead them. Kids could do that kind of work. Sometimes when our neighbor was plowing I went there and then when we plowed that girl came to our house to help. So I got to know her pretty well.

My swan-necked sweetheart
My blue-eyed girl

"Another woman was taken and kept chained to a wagon when the shepherd wasn't around. She had three children by the shepherd until the sheepherder didn't return for three days, which was unusual. She managed to have her oldest child bring some tools that were always kept beyond the length of her chain, she cut the chain and took the three children with her, back to her people."

Is there more?
There's always more, Mister.

When I was fifteen I was invited to a wedding. I sure was glad to go but I didn't have decent shoes. When we were kids we used a cloth shoe, and if it was muddy, a wooden one, so I needed a pair of leather shoes. Well my father didn't want to buy just dress shoes, so he bought me a heavy pair of work shoes. He was thinking that later I could use them in the fields and that way he could save money. They were awfully strong and they had lots of nails in the bottom, just like horseshoe nails.

Before then the only suit I ever had was for my First Communion, but it was too small. Mother took material from the coat and made the pants bigger. After I was all dressed up I felt pretty good, except for those shoes. They paired everyone off, boy, girl, boy, girl. They gave me a girl about three years older than I. But I was big for my age and she was happy with me all right. She was a very pretty girl.

Afterwards we went to a dinner and then there was a dance. She wanted to try it but I was kind of afraid. I was only fifteen and I didn't know how to dance yet, but I had an idea. We started dancing and all I could think about was those shoes. If I stepped on her feet I was going to mash them for sure. They were really noisy, too, "clop, clop, clop."

Two

AMERICA BECKONS

When I was twenty years old I began to make plans. One day I wanted to marry so I couldn't just stay as a hired hand. I knew I could get a girl but I didn't have any money and I didn't want to start like that. I didn't want to have to be like my father and buy my son shoes with nails instead of dress shoes. Somehow I thought I could do better.

If I married a girl and I had nothing and she had nothing, we were going to have a pretty hard time. One chance was to marry somebody who maybe had a little place already. My father did that, but that was hard, too. In the Basque country if the girl is the oldest, her parents give her one-quarter of the farm and they keep three-quarters. Then they live right there after you marry her. If you come with nothing her parents can tell you what to do. Lots of times there are no problems, but if you can't get along with the parents they can chase you away. The girl only owns one-quarter so she has to go with you. They pay her for the one-quarter and you are out.

I didn't want to hear the words, "You didn't bring anything here." I was thinking that if I had some money when I got married then I could buy another quarter interest in her farm from the parents. We would have half and they would have half, then they couldn't make us leave. If there was a problem maybe we could buy them out instead of the other way around.

I had my eye on two or three girls. One girl used to say, "Too bad you don't own a little property or I own a little property." I knew that my boss's older daughter liked me. She was only sixteen but if I wanted to wait she was going to marry me. There was another girl, too; she was working for my boss. She was two years older than me and she liked me all right. She had uncles and brothers in Argentina, and then she went there to live.

Well, I had that idea about earning some money before I married. I guess I really didn't have to because there were lots of farms that needed a strong young man like me, but my mind was made up. I decided the best thing was to go somewhere in America to work. I thought if I could save ten thousand francs then I would come back to Lasse and get married.[9]

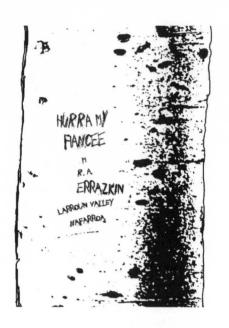

Scene 1: Take 1

Do you have to use all the lights and cameras?
It's for Euskal Telebista, The New York Times
Magazine! I already told you.
I forgot. You're gonna scare em.
We've got to have lights. Where's the other old
guy? Can we get them both?
Cut!
(Lights. Camera. Still less action)

> Garbi aitortzen dut ez nukela nahi
> Berriz astetikan asi.
> Gure nausiek lana eskeini
> jeki buruz gu etorri
> Emen sortuak baina euskaldunak.
> eta izena Etcheverry.
>
> I plainly confess I would
> not want to begin again.
> Our bosses offered us a job,
> that is why we came to them.
> They were born here but were Basques—
> And their name was Etcheverry.
> —Gratien Alfaro.

Cut!
Eh muchacho, why is this guy interrupting?
That's our bertsolari. He sings for his supper.
Did you know the president of Mexico was
Basque?
Luis Echeverria. My girlfriend's Garcia y
Echeverria.

(Aren't we all?)
Cut!

SCENE I: TAKE 2

> Elko Daily Free Press, Tuesday July 1,
> 2014: CORRECTION: The grand marshals
> for the 2014 National Basque Festival
> parade are Bartolo and Ramona "Eche-
> barria". Their name was misspelled in
> an article in Monday's edition of the
> Elko Daily Free Press.

What was Paradise really like, Señor ... Indiano?

————

Cut! Why won't he answer? This is for television!
You wanna hear the whole wild west story, do
ya, Mister? En vino veritas?
Claro que sí, of course. It's a documentary.

> LIFE Magazine, April 18, 1949.
>
> In January 1869 Elko consisted of two
> tents; by June of that year it was a
> busy, brawling, restless town of 2,000
> population. . .Silver had been discov-
> ered in the mountains to the south,
> and Elko was the nearest convenient
> point of the railroad. Almost at once,
> it became a booming supply and trans-
> portation center. When snow closed
> the roads to the mines, hundreds of
> miners, three-card monte dealers and
> women camp followers were cooped up
> in Elko's board shanties until spring.

> It was a "rather bad town", according
> to an early visitor. Shootings and
> killings took place daily. . . One of
> the town's more vicious pastimes was
> hanging Indian squaws to a flagpole
> in front of the first hotel.

Cut!

SCENE I: TAKE 3

Did you like the lamb, Señor? It's our house
specialty. You have garlic? You must get garlic.
Thanks, ok. What about the girl he left behind.
This Mari?

Cut!

SCENE I: TAKE 4

And what was the American woman?
Jane.

(Let's take dinner break everyone.)

SCENE 2: TAKE 1

Euzkalduna? You are Basque, French? the cineaste asked with two statements. Nonplussed and insistent, Navareese? ¿O español?
I wouldn't start out with that one, mister.
No? ¿Por qúe no?
He always says he's Americano-only. No Basque. No Spain. No France. No goddamned Catholic churches. A-mer-i-ca-no. Indiano solo.
Were you a cowboy or an Indian, Mr. Indiano?

> The Free Press: February 17, 1900 An
> old Chinaman known as "Cow Boy", was
> found dead in his dugout in Chinatown
> Saturday morning. He had probably
> been dead a couple of days. "Cow Boy"
> was quite a character and the Indians
> thought him half-crazy.

Scene 2: Take 3

> *Eskual Herritik jin nintzan*
> *hiru hogeita hiruan*
> *neguko lanbete inguruan*
> *urtarrilaraen hiruan.*
>
> *I came from the Basque Country*
> *in sixty three when*
> *winter chores were at their peak*
> *on the third day of January.*
>   Gratian Alfaro

Why is that guy squawking again? This is for
TV!
I told you. He's the bertsolari, our verse maker.
Can I get our Indiano to answer?
Worth a try.
Bueno. *Aita Zaharra*. How you feel about Amer-
ican woman?
He ignored me.
He does that.

> *Bi amoros xahar bero.*
> *Hirurogei-hamarra urtetan hartu die amorio*

He put the jukebox on again!
He likes that song.

Scene 2: Take 4

Who else you got for Euskal Telebista,
muchacho?
There's Quiroga.
Doesn't sound very Basque.
He's a Messican. No wait, maybe he's Peruvian.
I need Basque herders. This is Basque television.
I thought it was just old sipers you wanted.

Ai nere biotzeko begi urdindun Oh my blue-eyed girl

We need an American soundtrack for "The Last
Shepherd" documentary, country western, you
know."
How about Willy Nelson? *"Blue eyes cryin' in
the rain, Ai nere biotzeko begi urdindun."*
You got anything else? Retro-country?

I got another Marie one that's a Willie. We all
like Willie, even my Mari. Maria, shut up and
kiss me *Martitxu nora zoaz*? And it turns me on
and on *Nai ba-dezue etorri.*

——————

Want some jotas Navarras or somethin? We got
em all on the jukebox here: *Maitea Nun Zira/
Biskaia Maite/Lili Bat/Ama Eskondu . . .*
*On and on and on and on and on and on and on and
on and on and on and on and on and on and on and
Cut!*

SCENE 3: TAKE 5

¿Habla Ud. Español, Aita? (Does he speak any
Spanish? Know any English anymore?

> *Guk euskaraz / Zuk, zergaitik ez? Nik eta
> zuk / Egin behar dugu Euskal Herria Gure
> Buru*

He really likes that last part. He'll play it now.
We can't have an interview with the jukebox
playing that Basque stuff in the background.
This is a Western!

> *¿Erdera egiten ahal duzu? / Guk euskaraz /
> Gure buru!*

I told you he'd put it on again. He knows how
to trigger it in the back so he doesn't pay. That's
what he likes best.

Scene 3: Take 6

Did you ever want to go back to Euskal Herria, Monsieur?

> *Gizona, no duk zuurtzia*
> *Zer? Ez dakik*

What did that guy say?
Not my dialect. It's either about fate or a bush.
Don't you know Basque?
My Basque isn't that good either. Batua.
I thought you were from the Basque Country.
You're not Mexican, are you, Mister?
Mecaoenlaleche, how could I be Mexican if I come from the Basque Country?
How could I be Basque from Mexico?
Aren't you Mexican?
Quimosabe.
So you are or aren't Mexican, Chino-Juan Vasquez?
Puro Indio. Gure Aita Euzkal Herri'tik dator.
And your 'father' is from Basque Country and your mother from Mexico. How do you Americans say . . . you're a 'legal alien' then?
More alien than legal.
And who is your father?
Bertrand Indiano.
No te jode. The fuck you say.
We don't say that in Méjico, mister.

Scene 4: Final Take

Señor Indiano, por favor, what is your Christian name?

Agurjaunak

That song means he's done now. Bascos don't
talk much if they're not drinkin and he never drinks. They sing bertsos and carve trees in
the mountains. Maybe that's where you should
look, mister.

Dios mío, do all the stories end the same?
Ya know there's only two kinds a stories, donchya, mister?
Which are those?
Well, there's your cowboy-adventurer-dispos-
sessed hero story, and then ya got yer girl-left-
ya or yer somebody-dies-young tragic story.
(Personally, I think you should have a dog in
there somewhere too).
How about the drunk cowboy accidentally shoots
his dog inconsolable about the young girl with
consumption he left behind while singing story?

I can't handle the dog dying, mister. But, that's
me.

The Legend of Beltran Indiano

He was still a poor boy, and now he was alone.
He could not go back and Indiano had no sons.

Argi zagi edderra Argi egidazue!
Some suffering was beyond the telling. Ru- ru-run . . .
ruuuuuuuuuuuuuuuuuuuuuu!
Tskkkkts sugue Manu Ka Ka AHH éé yiiiii iiieeeEE! Aupá !
Ru-ru-ru-ru-ru-ru-ru
meeee-maaaa-meeee-maaa Pr-rr-r-r-r-r-r
eeehouuuuuuuuú! iiiiiiiiiiiiiiiiiiiiii
tSSSZZSSTSZZsstts kriskitin-sugea. . cascabeles

Manu thhe rattlesnake kxstkssst..!
TZXKSKSK tst s cocorico cu cu

Hell was the mountains.
Hell was the desert. But the real hell was other men.

Ka ka
Ka ka
Aru uu up

Ku ku ru ku. . .
Wa wa wa wa aruuu!! Basajauna!
Baaaaaaaaaaaaaaa aa a aaaaaaaaaa aaaaa a a aa aaaaaaaaaaaaaa
a aaaaaaaaaaaaaa. . .

I.

The shepherd boy comes down into town from the baserri, comes fresh off the farm running down the cobbled Rue de la Citadelle which winds its Renaissance way though the town houses of pink gray schist. St. Jean Pied-de-Port on the River Nive, gateway to the Pilgrim's Way. He reaches the Pont Eyerabaerri on his way to the plaza. *Gaur jaia!* Today, a festival day. Dantzara he goes to dance, to sing, to play *pilota*, handball in the *frontón* with the big boys until his hand reddens and swells. The boy goes to town today to fill his palm happily with fluid-pus, the fresh flesh rubbed raw. Today he is joyous. *Jaiera dantzera* on his sunshine way to wine and to dancing, on his way to singing and being young. But his way like scripture is set in sandstone: Tomorrow, he is off to a New World. His passage indentured, making him free. Today, this part of his journey is complete.

II.

Beltran had no family, no money, no home. For years on end, the sheep boss kept his wage. *An bero eta otz aundia.* Nevada was the worst of both worlds: hot as hell, cold as paradise. He was still a poor boy, and now he was alone. He could not go back, but Indiano had a dog.

How does your dog understand the commands, Mister?

He speak Basco.

Arrapatu, Txiki! Arrapatu! Go fetch.

Atzian jun! Get back der, meester!

Egon, Itzala. Stay stay.

Itzala, Shadow, he called her. He was lost within her topaz eyes. *Kipularen azala baina finao*, the tips of her ears were as smooth, as fine as the skin of an onion. Only he knew the soft furring of her paws, ebony turning metal gray then paler ash at the root of the pilpule. Only he knew her great pleasure as he scratched the rough scruff that curved where her shoulder blades met along the upper back at the base of her spine as she smiled. Shadow. Lady Nightshade. *Itzala egon.* Stay.

III.

Goddamned sheep had shit for brains

In the highlands there was pine, spruce, juniper, aspen—mountain mahogany, and lying there with his dog and the woolies in the great beginning of early spring, Indiano thought there could be no greater pleasure for a man than these Nevada mountains. The grasses were a high desert miracle pushing insistent up beneath the snow: fresh dew, wild white violets, columbine, he could smell them still! Blue lupine, Indian paintbrush—all yellow and red flash. The white snowflowers against the rain-drenched scent of morning sage could make a man cry if he let himself. *Bedar eder usaiña* to smell the spring grasses. *Auxe bizia.* And Beltran Indiano had a .30-30 and Beltran Indiano had a dog.

Fucking coyotes / Lamb dead Siestatime

The herder who didn't know the mind of his sheep and the will of his dogs was a dead herder. *Txiki! Beltza! Lina! Queenie! Itzalaaaaa!* This much was certain—a man needed a companion, no matter what. Alone in the mountains, out on the desert, the lone herder would soon learn that *txamisturik jota*—once taken by the sage—there was no turning back. The solitude would eat a man alive if he let it. They said sheep were stupid creatures, but a band of them together could be a force with which to reckon. The trick was getting up early before daylight to ride herd on the band, but not to be in too much of a hurry either or they'd scatter.

Deys like a woman, dem sheeps, old Bastien had said, *treat em good in the mornin or all day dere'll be hell to pay!*

A good sheepdog would keep the sheep from bunching up and trampling the feed; a good dog could save a sheep or the herder's own life.

If there is no hope of returning back home/three will be something left on the trees of America

Here in the new world, there was treachery and death, drought, black rainstorms, hail as hard as *pilota* balls. There was gangrene and gringos, lonesomeness and the black dog always standing by in the shadows; but back at camp, the evening of day awaited him—the settling of the dogs, the shepherd's tent, the warm fire. The herder lived for the sunset moment when he lifted the heavy iron lid off the Dutch oven pot breathing in its fragrant offerings: freshly butchered meat, garlic, onions, carrots and potatoes, fragrant sheepherder's bread. *Naikoa da* (precious little is enough) the herder always thought, shooting a thin stream of wine from the leather *xakoa* down his desert parched throat. If a man sought it out long enough, there was always shade from the high heat of day.

IV
The End of Days

After bathing him in rain and tears, Maria Garcia—the last serving girl of Echevarria—wheels the last herder from Room 123 out to the dining room *serbidora'ra* where he may take the afternoon sun by the window facing the Ruby Mountains which has always been his place. Her capable hands are the color of mountain mahogany, slim and strong as sweet Jesus. She is a woman who knows what there is to do and always gets it done.

Isharrez, pressing ever gently the cool cloth on the hot forehead of the last shepherd, *Aita, Father can you hear me?* she whispers. And he can. *O remember that my life is wind. Those are pearls that were his eyes, she says. Remember me. I will always remind you,* he replies.

Ait-tá-tá, the baby boy patters on, the dead man's hands clutching the precious flesh parceled by God.

Say *Ai-tá-tá Aitxi-txi-txa.* Hello Grandfather!

Ba baa ru-ru-ru-ru drool says the baby.

Ez kakin. Don't shit on me, says the herder in his head.

The Lord is my shepherd (The herder has found his voice again).

Arrapatúú! Go catch that Dirty Charlie coyotl, Itzala.

Toro! Tororororo! The running of the rams, he remembers.

Gure Aita, Our Father (neither of them knowing how much is left of him). *Zeruetan zarena* who art in heaven. *Hemen gire* here we are because we have come. We two with you. Your children Chino and Maria with our Kixmi. Helloo Grandfather! *Parkatu gora zorak* Forgive us our trespasses. . .

Ze diabru ari zera? What the hell you doin, gul? (Always the diaper). *He will not escape from darkness / The flame will wither his shoots.* Juan Chino y María. Now there with him together, hand-in-hand, the couple stand vigil on the shepherd's watch. As they glance back and forth—their son between them—they take what meaning they need from the rheumy white orbs of his eyes. *Pearls that were his eyes.* Father Joe offers the dry cadaver a wafer, then a drink from his paper cup.

(Take this). Maria, the mother, holds the withered old hand as the baby sleeps on peacefully in the wheelchair in the hotel in Paradise as the afternoon goes opaque.

Poor shepherd

From day until night you make an end of me.
    ¿Qué coño!? What-the-hells? *When do puppy doggies come with no furs, no teeths?* (The herder has found his voice again.)
    We call him Kixmi Indiano. He is our son, father. *Cu-cu-ru-cu-cu urtxo zuria* little white dove. *O remember that my life is wind.*
    (Oooh Chino, I think he farted).
    As we forgive those who trespass against us.. .Ai-tá-tá-tá ta. . . Itzala arapatuuuu! Go git em Shadow.
    Clutching the baby by the wings in the cradle of his mariner's hands, the ancient herder fashions a bird's nest of feathers and fluff and broken twigs for the boy

as shelter. *This is my blood.*

Maria Garcia Echeverria lifts the skeleton and in one swift, certain movement, removes the soiled dressing from his wither boned loins. She lifts the old torso like the fallen trunk of a slender quaken asp, his legs dangling from her clutch like broken branches. *Za-kil ma-kil ez i-ku-tú* you git you dirty hands off my shepherd staff or I murder you!

(*Ma-hi,* he whispers in rattlesnakes *cascabeles.*) Maria lifts the herder as he hisses, then alternately moans from the cavern hole toothless. *Gaiztolzuluetan.* She holds him careful, she holds him tender. *Ma-yiii,* his breath like wind in dry grass rasping. (This the miracle of my flesh.) *Then came from the heaven a noise like violent rushing wind.*

Sweet Jeezus, Chino, not again!

Act V

Argitzailean . . . within the vigil of light the ghosts have come for him. All is still—the dead they are listening. Now he is ours they whisper whisper

> *Agur Ma....ri....a gra...zias*
> *Hail Mary full of grace*

In the house of Echevarria at the last supper, they all watch and wait, keep the shepherd's watch waiting for it all to begin again. The young girl Mayi takes the brown paper sack of her betrothed, tearing him to skin and bones. His thin flesh is like a whisper. In the end, she tells him, *Ordu da.* Maitea, my darling, it is time. She hushes him weeping, puts the baby to her breast to suckle. *Ama, emaoiozu tittia. Lo lo lo xo. hush. Ordu da* the hour has come. Tells him gently: *Old man, you're out of time.*

Now Juan Vasquez (also called Chino) takes up the fragile frame of the old man, holds him under the shoulders, pulls him on up from the wheelchair, then gently pours dribbles of broth between the cracked lips hoping—*olio salda* hoping for a few days more.

Father, don't leave me. The white eyes like marble do not see him, but the rhythm of the young man's breathing tells him someone is near. *Shi-no*, the words have nearly left him. *My son* now only the singing. *Agur Ma ri a. Like a shepherd's tent my dwelling is pulled up and removed from me* . . . Take me, take me.

Mayi, the tree of your slender neck I am climbing. I gave you my word, Maitea. Where have you been? *Hemen duzu gure Shino.* Here, our Chino. *Ohikua nuzu.* He will take us all around town. *Kadillakaz* by black Cadillac! He will take us to Paradise, Mayi. Itzala is watching the sheep as we journey. *Nik ez zaitut ikusten / ez berririk jakiten / nurat galdu zera?* I still cannot see you. No news of you. *Ma Marie*, why did we wait a hundred years?

Farewell my darling

Mayi comes to him now dressed in gossamer and time, all about her the fast spell of chestnut tresses. She sees he is dressed for mass in his good hobnailed shoes and nods in agreement. *Ala ba-goaz.* It is time to go. *Regarde, regarde! Le feu de Saint-Jean, Mari!* The fires of midsummer's eve welcome us to Paradise, he cries out to the skies. *Suakau su zu zera.* They have lit the fires within the stone walls for you you, Maitea, my darling. The light of the solstice will guide us across the water today. Marie, I am coming to the opposite shore. *Mayi ba-nator!*

After feasting, after so long, it is Chino who puts the old songs on the jukebox for the last time. *Agur Jaunak. Aita Semeak.* Father and son are here in the tavern/Mother and daughter at play at home. Mayi lifting, Mayi weeping, raises him from the wheeled chair up on to the stone bench on the banks of the swollen river. Seated on that ancient bench she had listened to his first declaration of love, and there also had avowed what she felt to him promising herself. *Maitea nun zira / ni ez zaitut ikusten . . .*

Otz otz. He is so cold! *Xo xo ixil ixilik euria dator.* Hush, the big rain is coming. Stay with me, Mayi. Stay! I am with you. Do not be afraid. I have not forsaken you. *Ez nuzu kambiatu.*

At last, Itzala—the final visitor, enters like an honored guest. The dog's whiskers brush him like the wisps of a web as she comes to him, thief in the night. *Tori tori Itzala!* Come come. There in the shepherd's tent sheltered by the dove gray darkness, the dog pulls at the cuff of the herder's frayed shirt. *Itzala tentala dago.* It is dawn, time to go now. Itzala is waiting. The dog watches the flock. *Egon.* First, shyly, she nibbles daintily at the pearl white button snaps encircling the wrists like heaven, then tastes each finger languorously licking the bones. At last she snuffles ecstatically into the taut flesh of the palms with her soul and the last herder takes his last breath.

With the carcass now cracked open, the dog gnaws the knobby bones of each exquisite hand, then licks her black velvet lips as deeply she drinks. The arteries, veins and capillaries are sucked dry now leaving faint traces like wine in paper cups, like pink afterbirth. Itzala, the she wolf, has drank the blood of the herder now thirstily leaving behind little mess. *Comme désert*, sweet marrow from the bone.

In the final take, the black dog reaches the tendered flesh of the old man's neck and licks the collarbones like a lover. Then she stops for a moment considering the head, looking at last into the deadened eyes.

The Basque who was the herder they called Indiano had lived at Echevarria's so long his steak was seasoned with garlic. Beltran Indiano tasted like lamb.

Suscipe
Take me, take me.

I am Ramon

99520796R00150

Made in the USA
Columbia, SC
10 July 2018